"Are You Ready To Pay The Price?"

Kane asked softly, his hand snaking out to seize her wrist. Slowly, deliberately, he pulled her to him.

Carling held herself rigid, but his greater strength overcame her resistance. Against her will, she found herself inching toward him.

Frantically, she tried to take a step back, to put some much-needed distance between them, but it was too late.

"Go on and fight me, baby," he taunted huskily, his hard, muscular arms firmly anchoring her against him. "You know you want to."

"I do not! I'm hardly the fighting, spitting, scratching she-cat type, Mr. McClellan. If that's what you're looking for in a wife, I suggest you continue your search."

"My search for a wife has ended, Carly," he drawled. "When you go to bed tonight, you'll be Mrs. Kane McClellan."

Dear Reader:

Happy Holidays from all of us at Silhouette Desire! This is our favorite time of year, so we've pulled together a wonderful month of love stories that are our gifts to you, our readers.

We start out with *Man of the Month* Luke Branson in Joan Hohl's *Handsome Devil*, which is also a sequel to *The Gentleman Insists*, February 1989's *Man of the Month*.

Also, look for three wonderful stories filled with the spirit of the season: *Upon A Midnight Clear* by Laura Leone, *The Pendragon Virus* by Cait London and *Glory, Glory* by Linda Lael Miller. Rounding out December are the delightful *Looking For Trouble* by Nancy Martin and the tantalizing *The Bridal Price* by Barbara Boswell. All together, these six books might make great presents for yourself—or perhaps for a loved one!

So enjoy December's Silhouette Desire books. And as for 1991 . . . well, we have some wonderful plans in store—including another year of exciting *Man of the Month* stories! But more on all that in the new year. In the meantime, I wish each and every one of you the warmest seasons greetings.

All the best,

Lucia Macro
Senior Editor

BARBARA BOSWELL

THE BRIDAL PRICE

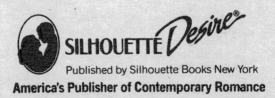

SILHOUETTE *Desire*®

Published by Silhouette Books New York

America's Publisher of Contemporary Romance

SILHOUETTE BOOKS
300 East 42nd St., New York, N.Y. 10017

Copyright © 1990 by Barbara Boswell

ISBN: 0-373-05609-5

First Silhouette Books printing December 1990

Printed in the U.S.A.

Books by Barbara Boswell

Silhouette Desire

Rule Breaker #558
Another Whirlwind Courtship #583
The Bridal Price #609

BARBARA BOSWELL

loves writing about families. "I guess family has been a big influence on my writing," she says. "I particularly enjoy writing about how my characters' family relationships affect them."

When Barbara isn't writing and reading, she's spending time with her *own* family—her husband, three daughters and three cats, whom she concedes are the true bosses of their home! She has lived in Europe, but now makes her home in Pennsylvania. She collects miniatures, holiday ornaments, tries to avoid exercise and has somehow found the time to write over twenty category romances.

One

"Carling, you have a visitor," Senator Clayton Templeton announced as he knocked lightly on his daughter's bedroom door. "It's Kane McClellan and he's waiting downstairs in the living room for you."

Carling was sitting in the window seat and staring blindly at the neat rows of tulips that filled the wide flower beds in front of the Templetons' Bethesda, Maryland, house. She tensed, but made no reply.

Through the closed door she heard her father clear his throat and murmur, "Don't keep him waiting, my dear."

Don't keep him waiting? Carling's mouth twisted into a scowl. It wasn't enough that she'd been forced into the position of slave on the auction block; she was also supposed to spare the bidder the inconvenience of waiting!

The force of her anger carried her out of her room and down the stairs, but a few steps short of the living room a sudden tidal wave of tension and anxiety brought her to an abrupt halt. Waiting inside was the man she was supposed to agree to marry. *A man she hadn't even dated*. She'd only met Kane McClellan a few times and very briefly at that, but she'd known in those short, infrequent moments that she didn't like him and never would.

Her stomach began to churn and her mouth went dry as the nervous tension escalated to panic. *Marry him?* The notion was positively medieval. She couldn't go through with it; there had to be a way out. Not only was being forced into an alleged "marriage of convenience" ridiculously archaic, not to mention horrifying, but Kane McClellan just wasn't her type in any way.

Physically, he was too big, too tall and too dark for her tastes. From what she knew of his life-style, it was too reclusive for an extrovert like herself. Even worse, he was aggressive and unyielding with a domineering streak a mile wide. She'd immediately picked up on that from the few words they'd exchanged during their mercifully quick meetings.

She had been told by her father that Kane McClellan owned a large cattle ranch several hundred miles from Dallas, and that he also possessed an unerring acumen for real estate and business investments, which had made him a very wealthy man. She'd heard McClellan described as a loyal, longtime Templeton supporter by members of her father's inner circle. Translated, that meant he was a generous financial contributor to Senator Clayton Templeton's campaign coffers.

Carling had managed to find out a little more about the man on her own and what she'd heard further convinced her that she had been absolutely right to turn down his invitation to dance at that Houston fund-raiser last summer, that her refusal to have dinner with him following a campaign rally on another evening in Dallas had been right on the mark.

Her father might admire Kane McClellan's wealth and financial prowess, but she'd seen no reason to further her own acquaintance with him. She'd learned that McClellan rarely left his ranch, preferring a reclusive life-style far from the glittering social world which she inhabited in Washington, D.C., where her father served as the senior senator from Texas. Kane was equally a stranger to the Texas social scene, while she was firmly established in both Dallas and Houston circles.

Carling peeked into the living room and saw Kane standing in front of Great-Grandmother Templeton's mahogany tea cart, on which an antique china tea set was placed. His presence seemed to dominate the elegant room and Carling inhaled sharply as the sight of him impacted on her senses.

His hair was straight and dark, almost coal-black in color, and was cut short in a style that would never require the upkeep of regular salon trims, hair dryers and sprays. If he needed a haircut he no doubt went into a barber shop, probably one with spittoons for the chewing tobacco habits of its patrons. The first time she'd met him, Carling had imagined him washing his hair with a bar of soap in the shower, toweling it dry, running a comb through it and then forgetting about it. A decidedly different attitude from many of the trendy, style-conscious men she knew.

His features were hard and sharp and as frankly masculine as the rest of him—the firmly set jaw, the sharp blade of a nose, the wide, sensual mouth and thick, dark eyebrows.

He was six foot four with a powerful masculine frame, broad-shouldered and muscular with a physique that radiated virility. He looked strong and powerful and she knew the image was in no way an illusion. He *was* strong and powerful. The one time he had touched her—that night in Houston when he'd taken her hand and asked her to dance—she'd felt the strength and power in his long, well-shaped fingers. She had refused him and for just a moment, before he'd let her go with a shrug and a smile, he had tightened his hold on her, making her irrevocably aware that had he chosen, he could have kept her with him for as long as he wanted.

A man of his size and strength could make her do anything he wanted her to do and for one unguarded moment, she had found that sheer, feminine helplessness intriguing. Shocked with herself, she'd quickly allowed outrage to prevail instead. The disconcerting episode had redoubled her determination to have nothing to do with the man. She was too independent, too used to having things her own way, to cede to the demands of any man.

She watched him pick up a small antique silver frame, which contained an old-fashioned baby picture of her grandmother. The delicate frame seemed dwarfed in his big hand. Carling shivered. Big. He was certainly that. The sheer size of him had an unnerving effect upon her, and she didn't understand why. She only knew that he made her feel wary and hostile, that he made her want to run in the opposite direction.

Her eyes flicked over him once more. He was as solid as a chunk of granite, she thought with a disparaging frown. And he was wearing jeans—*again!* He'd worn jeans every time she'd met him. Didn't he have anything else to wear? His jeans weren't the trendy, designer type that were the only kind worn in Carling's crowd. Kane McClellan's jeans were practical and well-worn. Carling's blue eyes widened. And he wore them well. They fit snugly in the front and back, molding his long, muscular thighs and tight buttocks in what she considered a thoroughly unnerving sex-defining way.

Deliberately, she dragged her eyes away from that mesmerizing sight, but her gaze remained riveted upon the rest of him. She took in his crisp blue chambray shirt and his pale sheepskin jacket. She was certain that the fine leather Western boots he wore were part of his everyday garb, and were not strictly worn to parties with a Western theme. Her well-trained shopper's eye recognized the enduring quality of his clothes—expensive but functional. He was the epitome of the authentic, moneyed working rancher.

She gulped. What was the matter with her? Anyone who might happen to come by and see her staring into the living room at him, would think she was ogling him. Which she most definitely was not! Carling Templeton did not ogle men in general, and in particular not an overbearing, barbarous cowboy, who was determined to ruin her life. Or her father's career...

"How long are you going to stand cowering in the hall?"

Carling started violently at the sound of the deep, slow drawl. Kane McClellan turned slowly to face her. She went hot and cold all over. He had given no indication that he'd been aware of her presence, but as his slate-gray eyes locked with hers, she knew at once that he'd known she had been there all along.

She felt a hot blush sweep over her from head to toe and silently cursed her fair coloring and her penchant for flushing when in the throes of strong emotion. "I wasn't cowering," she snapped. Carling Christine Templeton did not cower *or* ogle! "I was bracing myself for the horror of having to deal with you."

Kane carefully placed the picture back on the tea cart. "The horror of dealing with me?" he repeated. Unfortunately from Carling's point of view, he didn't seem at all offended by the jibe. Instead he smiled, as if he was amused.

He began to walk toward her, very slowly. She stood rooted to the spot, transfixed by his confident, lazy stride.

"You've assiduously avoided dealing with me in the past," he remarked in that gravelly, husky voice of his. "Does this mean that you've decided to accept my offer of marriage, Miss Templeton?"

She could tell by the gleam in his eyes that he was definitely mocking her. Carling seethed. "As if I had any choice at all, you—you snake!"

He was standing in front of her now and he was much too close. Excruciatingly aware of his virile size and strength, she found herself in the grip of an overwhelming need to turn and run. He was so close she could feel the heat emanating from his body. The scent of him, a combination of soap and a woodsy after-shave, filled her nostrils when she dared to inhale.

"You do have a choice," he said calmly. "You can marry me or not. The choice is yours to make, Carly."

"My name is Carling," she said coldly, stressing the pronunciation. "Since you're trying to force me into marrying you, the least you can do is to get my name right."

"I know your name," he replied with maddening affability. "I just prefer my own shortened version of it. A pet name, if you will." He took a lock of her champagne-blond hair between his fingers.

Carling froze. She felt unable to breathe, unable to move. His nearness, his touch seemed to immobilize every part of her body. Helplessly, she raised her eyes to his. Their gazes held as his fingers slowly rubbed the strand of hair in a patently suggestive way.

She abruptly jerked away from him, as if she'd been scalded. "I don't want or need a pet name from you! I'm not your *pet* and I resent your chauvinistic, demeaning, overbearing—"

"I get the picture," Kane interrupted dryly. "Let me amend my explanation. I prefer Carly because I'm too lazy to tack on those extra letters. And because Carling sounds like the name of a brewery to me."

Carling fumed. "It happens to be my mother's maiden name."

"My mother's maiden name was Lacey," he said, shrugging. "I'm forever grateful to her for not having bestowed it on me. Can you imagine the schoolyard brawls that were avoided by naming me Kane instead?"

"Except she spelled it wrong. It should be C-a-i-n, like that murderous fiend in the Bible."

He had the unmitigated gall to laugh. His refusal to argue with her was wildly frustrating. She wanted to see him furious and insulted, to make him storm from the house in a rage and never look back.

"Do you want an engagement ring?" he asked instead, in an infuriatingly amiable tone.

"No!"

"Then there's no need to waste time picking one out. We can be married immediately." He reached into the pocket of his sheepskin jacket and pulled out a small box, flipping the lid open to reveal a thick gold band. "Here's your wedding ring. Let's go."

"Go?" Carling paled. "Now? Oh no, we can't. It's— we—" she broke off as she realized she had lapsed into incoherence.

"We certainly can. Your father was kind enough to inform me about a place in Fairfax, Virginia, which condenses the usual three-day waiting period for a blood test and license into a few hours. He tells me that we can have a civil ceremony performed there."

"You must be pleased to have such an accommodating future father-in-law." Carling felt bitterness gnawing her like acid. Disillusionment shadowed her deep blue eyes. It was difficult to grasp and almost impossible to accept—that her father who for years had doted upon her, his only child, should now be so eager to literally *sell* her to this man.

"I like your father, both personally and politically," Kane said blandly. "I always have. He's been an excellent senator for our state and done more for the interests of the oil and gas industry than anyone in Congress. That's why I've always supported him."

"And you're such a fan that you're buying his daughter?"

Kane smiled. "Is that how you see it? That I'm buying myself a bride?" He didn't seem unduly perturbed by the notion.

"Yes! What's even worse is that you're blackmailing my father and me into going along with you!"

A wave of rage swept through her, so fierce that she began to tremble from the force of it. He was towering above her, so vibrantly male that he evoked some wild and primitive feminine response from deep within her. But she refused to acknowledge it. She hated the man.

Kane shrugged. "I'm not blackmailing you, sweetheart. If you don't want to marry me, all you have to do is to tell me no and I'll leave."

"As if it's that easy!" Her voice rose. For the first time in her life she truly understood the phenomenon of "seeing red," as a rosy haze of fury swam before her eyes.

"My father owes you hundreds of thousands of dollars. He'd have to declare bankruptcy and even then he couldn't repay you. And—and it's illegal for a senator to accept such large sums of money in the first place. You have my father and me backed against the wall and you know it!" She felt her eyes fill with tears as depression abruptly replaced her anger.

Last night's scene with her father replayed vividly in her mind. They'd had another argument and she had gone to her room dispirited. For the past two years she and her father seemed to do nothing but argue, and she was confused and heartbroken by the change in their previously loving and mutually admiring relationship. Worse, the argument always centered on the same topic: Carling's unwillingness to marry a wealthy young man and give her parents the grandchildren they craved.

Or that they claimed to crave. Last night the senator, looking older than his usual debonair sixty years, had confessed the truth. As much as the Templetons wanted grandchildren, they wanted—they *needed!*—a wealthy son-in-law.

Carling had listened in stunned silence as her father confessed that the life she'd been living had all been a lovely fantasy fostered by the illusion that the Templetons were as rich as everyone else in their tri-city social circles. For the first time Carling learned that they were not at all rich; they merely lived well, relying on the senator's honorariums and the largess of his constituents and friends to supplement his congressional salary, while stretching credit to the limits and beyond.

Carling's mother, Neva, had never worked, but she loved to shop. Her exquisite taste was evident in her wardrobe and the family's two large homes, in Bethesda and in Dallas, as well as in the family apartment in Houston. Carling, at twenty-eight, had never worked for pay, either. There had never been any reason to. Occasionally helping out in her father's office, making public appearances during his various reelection campaigns, and her charity fund-raising work had always been her full-time occupation—along with socializing.

The senator hadn't confided his financial worries to his "girls," as he fondly referred to his wife and daughter. Instead, he'd opted to try his luck in the stock market and bought a lot of stocks on margin. Two days ago, his broker had called with devastating news: the stocks were dropping and a huge margin call payment needed to be made at once. Clayton Templeton didn't possess the necessary cash resources to cover the payment, which was so large that he would lose everything he owned.

Desperately, he'd called upon the man who had easy access to such substantial sums, the man who had been expressing a keen interest in Carling for well over a year: Kane McClellan.

Kane had readily agreed to cover the sum for the stocks, the senator told Carling, and she had blanched at her father's words. She'd been savvy in the way of politics since her teens; she knew that the Federal Election Act limited the amount of money that politicians were allowed to accept in campaign donations or personal loans. The amount Kane McClellan had paid for those stocks far, far exceeded that limit, making her father liable for an ethics investigation by the Senate and possible prosecution for accepting illegal loans.

And this was an election year! Carling thought of the other party's candidate for the senate seat, a young man who had managed to garner a surprising amount of statewide support. As things stood, Clayton Templeton's reelection was probably assured, but an ethics investigation and financial scandal could easily swing voters to the opposition.

His position as a senator from Texas was her father's life, his entire identity! Carling couldn't fathom how he would handle losing his career, along with his social status and prestige. And her mother! They would have to sell their houses and all the beautiful furnishings, the priceless antiques and objets d'art Neva Templeton so enjoyed collecting. Carling shuddered at the thought of her mother trying to cope with both the loss and the scandal.

Feeling as if her heart had turned to stone, Carling had listened to her father propose the only way out, a plan which required her cooperation. At least, that's how her father had described it. Offering herself as a human sacrifice was closer to the mark, Carling thought.

If Carling were to marry Kane McClellan, any threat of Senator Clayton Templeton standing in violation of the Federal Election Act would be eliminated. There was no law limiting the amount of personal gifts or loans an elected official could accept from a member of his family, her father explained with pathetic eagerness. And wonder of wonders, McClellan was willing to forget the loan entirely and personally absorb the financial loss himself—*if Carling were to marry him.*

Now Kane McClellan was here to collect his prize—the bride he had purchased. Carling felt tears of fear and anger burning behind her eyelids and tried to blink them away. She would not cry in front of this—this atavistic savage!

"Why are you doing this?" she whispered, staring disconsolately at the floor. The brilliant patterns in the Oriental carpet blurred in her teary gaze. "Why in the world would you want to marry me?"

"I turned thirty-five last month," he said simply, dispassionately. "It's time I settled down and started a family of my own. I've devoted the past twelve years to building up the ranch as well as various other business interests. Now I want to share my life and fortune with a wife and children.''

"But what does that have to do with me?" Her voice cracked with desperation, but she pressed on, now determined to reason with him. "Surely you can find a woman who *wants* to marry you. Texas is a huge state and you're—'' she paused and gulped "—you're not an unattractive man. And, of course, you're very rich. That's certainly a lure to some.''

"Yes, isn't it?" he interjected dryly. "An irresistible lure, in some cases.''

She thought of her father who had been pushing the idea of her first meeting, then dating, now *marrying* Kane McClellan strictly on the basis of his financial status. Her flush deepened as shame rippled through her. But that was her father's doing, not hers! she reminded herself. She couldn't let Kane embarrass or intimidate her into giving up her fight!

"There must be some nice young woman out there who would be glad to be your wife and—uh—raise a family for you.'' She bit her lip, afraid that she'd sounded insultingly patronizing. She hadn't meant to, she merely wanted him to realize his options.

Kane shrugged nonchalantly, but there was nothing simple or dispassionate or nonchalant in the fires burning in his gray eyes. His gaze was hot enough to melt steel. "But I want *you*, Carly. For my wife, for the mother of my children.''

The uncompromising finality in his tone made her gnash her teeth in frustration. "That's ridiculous! We don't even know each other.''

"We'll have plenty of time to get to know each other after we're married. It's going to work out very well between us, Carly,'' he added, his voice firm with that promise.

An involuntary whimper escaped from her throat.

"I'd seen pictures of you before we met,'' he continued. "You're a knockout. Great big blue eyes, high cheekbones, a beautifully shaped, sexy mouth, plus all that blond hair. The only reason I attended those fund-raisers for your father was to meet you. I thought to myself 'here is a woman who has it all—beauty, brains, class.'" He smiled a heart-stoppingly sexy smile. "Not to mention a great body. Do you want me to rhapsodize about your breasts and your legs and that sweet little butt—"

"No!" she interrupted, her face scarlet. "You're unspeakably rude, Mr. McClellan. Rude and crude and sexist and—"

"Assaulted by adjectives," Kane interrupted dryly. "I'm none of the above, Carly, but I am honest and outspoken. You'll always know where you stand with me."

"You'll always know where you stand with me, too! At the top of the list of people I detest."

"Right now, you probably do think you hate me," he conceded. "But you'll get over it."

"I will not!" Carling suppressed the urge to scream, regretting that she'd been raised to view such unbridled exhibitions as unladylike. She was getting nowhere in her attempts to fight with Kane McClellan, she admitted ruefully. Her barbs didn't come close to penetrating his thick hide or daunting his incredible ego. He'd obviously decided that he was not going to allow her to drive him away. She must find another way to make him want to be rid of her as much as she wanted to be rid of him.

"So I'm supposed to believe that you fell in love with me from my photographs?" she demanded scornfully. She was infuriated that her heart was thundering faster and louder than a speeding train. "Only a naive, moronic fool looks at a picture of a woman and decides to marry her. An apt description of yourself, Mr. McClellan? Or maybe you're so socially inept and so totally devoid of personality that the only way you could ever get a woman to marry you is to buy her?"

"I'm sure you'll understand if I don't agree with either of those theories," he replied smoothly. "Try looking at it this way, Carly. What red-blooded male wouldn't want a woman with your face and body? If you like, you could choose to view the situation as wildly romantic—your besotted suitor going to extraordinary lengths to win the woman of his dreams. Because once I'd met you, I decided that you were the woman I wanted for my wife.''

His amused confidence set her teeth on edge. He hardly sounded like a besotted, romantic suitor. Unfortunately, he didn't exactly fit into the fool or social clod categories, either. He looked and sounded shrewd and hard and calculating, a man used to getting what he wanted. And he wanted her.

"Are you crazy?" Carling's voice rose. If things went on as they were, she might end up screaming after all, etiquette be damned. "The few times we met, I was horribly rude to you. I played the role of the snotty society bitch to the hilt!"

"I know." His gray eyes glittered. "You were very, very wary of me, weren't you, Carly? You still are. I might not be one of those fancy playboy types you like to party with but I certainly recognize sexual tension, and it's been vibrating between you and me from the moment we met. Right from the start you've been very aware of me and very eager to antagonize me, to fight with me."

"That's because I don't like you," she shot back furiously. "Oh, why bother to sugarcoat it? The truth is I hate you! And not only are you a blackmailing barbarian, you're self-deluded to the point of no return. The so-called *sexual tension* you've imagined in me is—is—really suppressed nausea."

"I see." He had the nerve to laugh at her and to cup her shoulders with his big, warm hands.

Carling stiffened. "Don't touch me," she warned in a voice that was not as commanding as she would have liked.

He didn't release her. "You're very skittish," he observed, arching his dark black eyebrows. "That's another thing I've noticed about you. You're too nervous for a woman who is accustomed to being touched by a man. That leads me to assume that you've kept your relationships with all those men you've been linked on a strictly platonic level.''

She was aghast that he'd hit on the truth. She did not like sex. The one time she had tried it, at the age of eighteen after a college fraternity party, had been quite enough for her. She and her date—whom she'd never spoken to again—had both had a bit too much to drink and the volatile combination of adolescent hormones, alcohol and curiosity had led to the mutual loss of their virginity. The memory was a distant one, but still repugnant to her.

Never had she experienced anything so painful and messy, so clumsy and humiliating. She had decided then and there never to do it again, and she hadn't. Nor had she ever had any trouble sticking to her vow. She'd earned a reputation for coolness—her detractors, frustrated with her icy unresponsiveness, had amended cool to frigid—but that didn't bother Carling. She didn't like being touched and she didn't care who knew it.

Until now. She did not like Kane McClellan knowing. It made her feel vulnerable, which alarmed her. Whoever said that knowledge was power had a point; having Kane know about her aversion to sex gave him a power over her and she hated it. Oh, how she hated him!

''You have one hell of a lot of nerve assuming anything about me, Kane McClellan!'' she snarled. She was well aware that a lady never cursed in the presence of a gentleman, let alone cursed the gentleman himself, but doing so was inordinately satisfying. And Kane McClellan was not a gentleman, anyway. ''Now take your hands off me this instant.''

He merely laughed, unperturbed by either her cursing or her command. ''It's time for you to get used to having my hands on you, honey. Because after we're married I'm not going to keep them off you. You'll soon become very accustomed to a man's touch. My touch.'' He pulled her closer with such strength that she was unable to pull away. "And you'll be much calmer and more content when you've worked off all that high-strung, nervous energy in bed with me."

"No!" she cried, nearly choking at the panic roiling inside her. "You can't do this. I won't let you! I won't marry you. I'll pay you back every penny you lent my father! Please don't make—" Her own fierce pride abruptly silenced her. She had been on the verge of pleading with him! Never would she sink to that!

"You're working yourself into a world-class bout of hysteria," Kane pointed out and his air of calm was in dramatic contrast to her frantic loss of composure.

Her resentment heightened. "I have a right to be upset, dammit! I'm living every woman's worst nightmare! You want to force yourself on me and—and hurt me and—"

"I'm not going to hurt you or force you in bed, Carly," he said quietly.

She was breathing heavily and her blue eyes were huge as she stared up at him. "You—you mean that if I marry you, you won't expect me to—to have sex with you?" For the first time since last night, she felt a flicker of hope. If there was no way out of marrying him, at least she might be spared the mortification of sleeping with him.

"My uptight little darling, you're incredibly naive if you think I'd ever consider a celibate marriage, particularly with you." His smile was predatory, provocative and fairly brimming with sexy male confidence. "But maybe it's time to show you that you have nothing to be afraid of concerning the physical side of our marriage. There'll be no forcing or no hurting. You'll give yourself to me and I'll satisfy you completely."

The way he was looking at her... those lazy gray eyes of his... the soft, seductive words... Carling felt frissons of heat rippling through her, which paradoxically made her shiver.

"The only way you'll ever be able to satisfy me is to disappear from the face of the earth," she cried fiercely, hating the peculiar, unfamiliar shakiness in her limbs, the tight knots which were coiling deep in her abdomen, the wild racing of her heart. Nobody else had ever evoked these strange, primitive sensations and she hated them, hated that they were beyond her control, hated that Kane McClellan could do this to her.

"Oh, I don't think so. I think you're about to realize that you are as hungry for me as I am for you."

Two

His hands slid possessively over her. With one hand at the small of her back and the other between her shoulder blades, he molded her against him with effortless expertise. Carling gasped at the contact of his hard, muscled body and instinctively began to struggle.

Kane merely tightened his grip, rendering her efforts to free herself useless. "I've heard you're called the Ice Princess," he said softly, his mouth just an inch above her own, his warm breath mingling with hers.

She felt helpless and dizzy, fighting the almost overpowering urge to close her eyes and relax against him. Instead, she held herself tautly and glared at him with furious, disparaging blue eyes.

But Kane was undaunted. "All that anger is masking the passion that you've managed to freeze inside you," he taunted, brushing his lips lightly against her own. "It's going to be as explosive as a nuclear meltdown when you finally let yourself unleash it."

The touch of his mouth, brief and light as it had been, electrified her. Alarm bells seemed to go off in her head, and in a renewed attempt for freedom, she managed to lever her hands against his chest and push at him with her palms.

"Nuclear meltdown? Spare me the ridiculous hyperbole." She was irked that she couldn't seem to raise her voice above a whisper, but pleased that she was still able to insult him. She would *not* succumb to his barbarian physicality like some addle-brained twit straight out of those daytime television programs she occasionally—and accidentally, of course—tuned into watch.

"You're a brute and a bully and I promise, I *swear* that I'll never, never ever—" She paused, searching for the words, her face crimson with outrage.

"Give into me?" Kane suggested. "Respond to me? Enjoy making love with me? Is that what you're having such trouble trying to say?"

"Yes!" Carling gasped hoarsely. "That's what I'm trying to say. I'll never willingly give into you. You'll have to resort to rape because I won't respond to you. I'll never willingly have s-sex with you."

Their gazes clashed and for one tense, silent moment they stared deeply into each other's eyes. Carling saw the gray flames burning there, saw his pupils dilated with desire. She felt the powerful strength of his thighs hard against her, was excruciatingly aware of her breasts crushed against his chest.

"Is that what you think, my little fire-and-ice princess?" His voice was deep and husky.

A sudden tremulousness made her feel weak and soft inside. She fought against it. Clenching her hands and abandoning any attempts at propriety, she began to hit him.

Kane's hold was inexorable. He didn't let her go, he held her closer and buried his lips against the slender, graceful curve of her neck. She felt him nibbling the sensitive skin with his teeth, then soothing it with his lips. She whimpered. She wasn't used to being touched or caressed, and the

surge of intense sensation rioting through her was both terrifying and darkly thrilling.

"Stop!" she demanded thickly. "Let me go!" Somehow
her fists had become uncurled and her hands inched slowly
to his shoulders. To push him away, Carling assured herself. His muscles rippled beneath her palms and her fingers
gripped him.

Kane lifted his head and laughed softly. "No, baby, I
won't let you go. I have you right where I want you at last.
You're finally where you belong and soon enough you'll
know it and admit it, to me and to yourself."

Outraged, she began to struggle again, but his superior
size and strength easily kept her his captive. He wouldn't
even let her hurt herself fighting him; he simply held her
tightly until she exhausted herself and lay limply against
him, gasping for breath.

And then slowly, his gray eyes glittering, Kane lowered his
mouth to hers. Carling watched with a passivity she found
appalling but couldn't seem to shake. He curled his hand
into her hair and he held her head still as his mouth opened
over hers and took possession of her lips.

His mouth was hard, hungry, demanding. He thrust his
tongue into her mouth in an excruciating sexual simulation
of what he intended to do with her body. Carling began to
shake. Her mouth was open under his and she sampled the
hot heady taste of him as she helplessly accepted the slow
penetrating thrusts of his tongue.

He was so big, so strong; the masculine sound and smell
and shape of him surrounded her. She felt her breasts swell
and their sensitive peaks tighten as arrows of fire burned
from her belly to the moist, secret place between her legs.
Carling quivered.

She tried to tear her mouth from his, but his hold on her
was inexorable. She had no choice. She couldn't get away.
She had to stay in his arms with his tongue buried deeply in
her mouth as his big hands moved over her possessively,
gliding over the rounded curves of her bottom and posi-

tioning her intimately against the cradle of his iron-hard thighs, rubbing her, touching her.

Suddenly, she couldn't seem to stand. Her knees were too rubbery to hold her and she literally had to cling to Kane for support.

She wanted to scream, she wanted to faint. But she did neither. She was trembling and her body throbbed in response to the erotic rhythm of his movements. Neon lights were flashing in her head and she felt all coherent thought begin to slip away.

When his hand covered her breast in a gesture of pure male possession, she uttered a wild little cry from deep in her throat. His thumb traced the tight nipple beneath her teal-blue silk blouse, and seemingly of its own volition, her body arched against him.

And then, one disorienting moment later, it was over. He lifted his mouth from hers and his hands moved from their intimate positions on her breast and bottom. He stopped caressing her and held her tightly, but quite chastely, against him. "Someone's coming," he murmured against her ear. "Calm down, darling. Relax. We'll continue this tonight."

His words exploded in her head like a bullet to the brain. "No!" she cried, and she struggled against him.

To her surprise and infinite relief, he let her go. "No, you won't calm down or no, you won't relax?" Somehow he managed to look and sound both seductive and satisfied at the same time.

Carling longed to smack that smile of amused male confidence from his face. "I mean, no, we won't continue this tonight."

She wanted to melt into a puddle of pure embarrassment when he laughed softly and murmured, "Oh, yes, sweet. We're definitely going to pick up where we left off and you're going to be with me all the way."

Given her shocking performance in his arms, he probably felt quite justified in making his smug prediction. Carling suppressed the urge to wail in horror. Why hadn't she fought him tooth and nail? It must have been because he had caught her completely off guard; since she hated this man, there could be no other reason. He was everything she'd never wanted in a date, let alone a husband, yet something perverse and unpredictable inside her had nearly succumbed to his primitive sexuality.

Nearly? A nasty little voice in her head mocked her. She often heard and then firmly suppressed that voice because it inevitably made observations she didn't care to acknowledge. *Honey, you melted like wax in the sun and he hadn't even begun to turn up the heat. Wait until tonight, when he does...*

"Well, well, look who's here!" The clear oratorical tones of Senator Clayton Templeton sounded from the staircase, filling the foyer.

Carling whirled to face her smiling parents, who were descending the stairs together. While the senator was pulling off a credible impression of being surprised to see Kane McClellan in his home, his wife was genuinely so.

Carling knew that her mother was unaware of the senator's disastrous financial plight and Carling's impending fate. When Clayton Templeton had made his desperate confession and plea the night before, he'd begged his daughter not to mention a word of it to her mother. Carling, heartsick, panic-stricken and filled with dread, had agreed. After all, she'd reasoned glumly, why should her mother have to feel this way, too?

"Neva, you remember Kane McClellan, of course," Clayton boomed heartily, as they joined the younger couple. "He's a tried-and-true Templeton supporter from the Triple M Ranch southwest of Dallas. You've met him at some of the rallies..."

His voice trailed off. All three Templetons were fully aware that Neva mainly knew Kane McClellan as the man that the senator was forever trying to interest Carling in— the man whom Carling vociferously refused to have anything to do with. Yet here the pair stood in the hall. Carling's usually impeccably coiffed blond hair was sexily mussed and her lips slightly red and swollen, most definitely from being kissed. Carling saw her mother's eyes widen in confused amazement.

"We're very pleased to welcome you to our home, Mr. McClellan," Neva said, recovering quickly, her ingrained hospitality and never-failing political instincts carrying her through whatever private thoughts she might be harboring. "Carling dear, have you offered our guest some refreshments?"

"Oh yes," Kane said politely. The gleam in his gray eyes was positively wicked. "Thanks to Carling, I'm definitely refreshed."

Carling glowered at him. The charade was becoming unendurable—her father pretending that he hadn't arranged for Kane McClellan to be here, that he hadn't set the wheels in motion for Carling's ignominious plunge into slavery! And just when she thought she couldn't stand it for another moment, it got worse.

"Senator, Mrs. Templeton, I'd like to ask for the hand of your daughter in marriage," Kane interjected smoothly. "I've discussed it with Carling and she has agreed to do me the honor of becoming my wife. Having your blessing would mean the world to both of us."

Carling balled her hands into fists. Was she the only one to recognize his gallant-sounding words were spoken strictly tongue in cheek? She glared at him fiercely, and he countered by reaching over to grab her hand and holding it firmly in his. His eyes challenged her to contradict him, dared her to pull away and order him out of her house, out of her life.

Of course she didn't. And unless she wanted to bankrupt her family and kill her father's career, she was in Kane's power and they both knew it.

Her mother gaped at Kane, obviously dumbfounded by the news. After all, the last Neva Templeton had heard from Carling was that Kane McClellan was uncivilized and antisocial, an appalling throwback to some Neanderthal ancestors, and that she'd rather date a gorilla. "Carling, this is so—so—*so unexpected,*" Neva managed to say at last.

Kane grinned. "I believe Carling has said that nothing in the world could induce her to date me," he said cheerfully. "But it seems like marrying me is an entirely different matter."

"Indeed it is!" Senator Templeton exclaimed, reaching for Kane's other hand and shaking it heartily. He turned jovially toward his wife. "Neva, my dear, I hope you'll forgive this little deception of ours. You see, Carling and Kane let me in on their secret romance weeks ago and I convinced them to wait and surprise you. If you'll look at the Style section of this morning's *Post,* you'll see their engagement announcement, which I took the liberty of sending in."

"What?" Carling and Neva chorused.

"I've ordered several thousand copies to be delivered to the house later today," Clayton continued. "I want my staff to send clippings of the announcement to all our closest, dearest friends."

"Your closest, dearest friends number in the thousands?" Kane asked dryly.

The senator nodded, oblivious to the irony in Kane's tone. His sarcasm, however, hadn't eluded Carling. Her lips tightened as she glared at her newfound fiancé. She was equally upset with her father. Obviously he had been certain enough of her capitulation to mail an engagement announcement to *The Washington Post!*

She thought of the sad little scene last night, of her father's seemingly hopeless and pitiful despair. Since the announcement that would save his skin had already been prepared for publication, had his tears simply been a masterful piece of acting?

"Welcome to the family, Kane, my boy," the senator exclaimed expansively. "Nothing could make me happier than to see my little girl married to you!"

Truer words had never been spoken, Carling thought grimly. She swallowed back the protest of fury and indignation, which had welled up inside her, and turned her sapphire-blue eyes on her mother, silently willing the older woman to recognize her misery, to acknowledge that something very strange was going on and to demand an explanation.

Carling knew that there was only one person in the world from whom Senator Templeton would take orders and that was his wife, on the infrequent occasion she chose to issue them. If her mother were to learn of the mess they were in, if she were to forbid Carling to marry Kane McClellan just to bail them out of it . . .

Carling's heart leaped with hope. Oh Mama, please, say something! she mentally pleaded.

"This is such a surprise, I'm practically speechless, Kane," Neva exclaimed. She averted her eyes from the intensity of her daughter's gaze and turned her full attention to Kane. "And anybody who knows me knows that I'm seldom at a loss for words. Usually I have too many of them," she added with the charming frankness that had endeared her to countless voters, year after year.

"Well, I was surprised too, at first," the senator added quickly. "We kept singing your praises, Kane, but we didn't think our little girl was listening. Carling is so headstrong and independent that once she makes up her mind about something or someone it's usually impossible to make her change it."

He turned to beam at Carling, his voice utterly convincing in its sincerity. "You didn't want to tell your mama and me that you were secretly seeing Kane because you didn't want us to tease you or have to listen to us say I-told-you-so, isn't that right, my angel?"

Kane arched his eyebrows and made no comment, but Carling suspected he was secretly doubling over with laughter. In her opinion, her father was laying it on a tad too thick. What made it even worse was that three out of the four people standing here knew the truth!

"Carling certainly had us fooled," Neva said in a rather dazed voice. "She actually had us believing that she didn't want anything to do with you, Kane."

"The little minx," Kane said, his lips twitching with unconcealed mirth.

Carling wanted to smack him. She settled for shooting him a scathing look. "Mama, I believe my exact words were 'I'd rather date the gorilla in the National Zoo than Kane McClellan.'"

"Why, yes." Neva chuckled. "And now look, you're marrying him!"

"Maybe the gorilla was already spoken for," suggested Kane.

The senator and his wife laughed appreciatively.

"And he has a sense of humor, too!" Neva exclaimed, her eyes bright with delight. "Your young man is quite a catch, Carling. I'm thrilled to pieces for you. And for him, too, of course. And you're certainly going to make him a wonderful wife. Why, I'm thrilled for all of us!"

"So am I!" the senator added fervently.

Carling guessed that as the bride-to-be, she was supposed to make some sort of giggly, deliriously happy remark. She did not. She might be selling her body, but she would not sell her soul.

Her parents were too caught up in their own rapture to notice the lack of her own. "When can Carling and I begin planning the wedding?" Neva asked enthusiastically. "Oh, there is so much to do! But first things first—the engagement party! I'll call the Congressional Country Club right this minute and reserve the—"

"No need to do that, Neva," Kane cut in. His tone, ever polite, was also unmistakably firm. "Carling and I are skipping all the engagement hoopla. We're getting married immediately. Today, in fact. We're leaving for Fairfax, Virginia, right now."

Neva's giddiness was deflated as quickly as a balloon that had been pricked with a pin. "Oh." It was more of a gasp. "I—I see." She looked at Carling, and for the first time since the news of the marriage had been announced, she seemed to actually see her.

And Carling made no attempts to disguise her unhappiness, her anxiety and her nervousness.

"That place in Fairfax," Neva said, frowning. "That marriage mill where people who *have* to get married go immediately. Oh, Carling, at your age! And after all those years we attended the Planned Parenthood fund-raising balls! Now I truly am speechless."

Carling was appalled her mother thought she was pregnant out of wedlock at the age of twenty-eight! Her gaze flew to Kane and she blushed furiously. As if she'd let this reclusive brute from a cattle ranch take her to bed and make her pregnant!

"Mother, how could you believe such a thing even for a moment!" she cried indignantly.

"Don't be upset with your mama, sweetheart," Kane interjected soothingly. He casually swung one arm out and caught her around the waist, pulling her back against him, effortlessly, like someone reaching out to pick up a doll. But his arm was a steel band around her, holding her to him, an inexorable bond from which she couldn't break free or wriggle out of—though she tried to do both.

"I can see where your mother might misunderstand our haste," he continued, lowering his head to brush Carling's temple with his lips. "But let me assure you, Neva and Clayton, that my intentions toward your daughter are honorable and always have been, and I would never—" he paused and cleared his throat—choking back a laugh, Carling was sure "—sully her spotless reputation by anticipating our wedding night. Carling is definitely not pregnant now, but I hope she will be by this time next month."

Carling's heart plummeted and her stomach jumped, causing a dreadful upheaval in her middle. If she'd been made of weaker stuff, she would have burst into tears on the spot.

Instead, she tried to pry his arm from around her waist as she bared her teeth in a poor imitation of a smile. "Since we've cleared up that misunderstanding, let's rethink the entire Fairfax idea. If Mama has her heart set on giving us an engagement party and a big, fancy wedding, I certainly don't mind—"

"But I do mind, honey," Kane interjected. "I don't want to wait months while the wedding plans are in the works. Seems like a colossal waste of time to me. I want to take you home as soon as possible. It's settled, we're getting married today."

Though Carling burned to refute him, to refuse him, she stayed silent. She had no choice, and they both knew it. Kane McClellan was the one in charge and what he said, went. They both knew that, too. Like a master puppeteer, he controlled the strings and the Templetons, like marionettes, danced to his command—or else.

Carling and her father and Kane himself all knew what the unspoken but inevitable "or else" would be: the financial and political ruin of Senator Clayton Templeton and the public disgrace of the Templeton family. Carling looked at her mother, whose face was a study of confusion and concern, and tried to imagine the toll that such a scandal would have upon her.

The gossip, the gleeful speculation, the hounding by the media would forever change the pleasant, privileged existence which Neva Carling Templeton had enjoyed for all of her fifty-five years. As for Carling's father... well, she'd already spent hours agonizing over his fate if she were not to come to his rescue. She might be furious with him for putting her in this position, disillusioned with him for using her in this way, but he was her father. She loved him and would do whatever she could to help him. There was no use thinking about it anymore, no use looking for a way out.

She had to accept it. She was going to marry Kane Mc-Clellan today—in a quickie, impersonal marriage mill because his wish was literally her command.

Carling swallowed hard. "I guess we're on our way to Fairfax then," she said bleakly. Her acting talent didn't extend to pretending that she was happy. She turned her head slightly to look up at Kane, although she assiduously avoided meeting his eyes. "If you'll let me go, I'll get my jacket and purse and we can leave."

"Of course, sweetheart." Kane smiled. But before he released her, he dropped a quick hard kiss on her mouth in an unmistakable brand of possession. She shivered.

"Hurry back to me," he said. He deceptively made it sound like a request. Carling knew it was an order.

Her face flushed and blue eyes glittering, Carling raced up the stairs at a most unladylike breakneck speed.

Kane's eyes followed her until she reached the top and disappeared from view. He flicked his gaze to Senator and Mrs. Templeton, who were watching him uneasily. He read regret and wariness in the senator's eyes, curiosity and corresponding wariness in Neva's. He treated them to his most confidence-inducing smile. "There's nothing to worry about," he said reassuringly. "Everything is going to be all right, I promise you."

The senator nodded nervously. "Of course, we know that. It's just that—that—Carling is our little girl." His voice broke and he took a deep breath in an attempt to regain his composure. "We—Neva and I—have always wanted the best for her."

"I understand. I'm going to take good care of her," Kane assured him. "Perhaps she isn't too happy with the idea of this quick wedding, but she will be content and secure married to me."

"We've always dreamed we would give her a grand wedding with all the flourishes," Neva said mournfully. "Carling in a stunning white gown and bridal veil, Clayton walking her down the aisle of the National Cathedral, a wonderful reception at the club with all our friends..." Her voice trailed off.

There was a long moment of silence. Kane guessed that he was now supposed to allow the Templetons to produce the kind of wedding extravaganza that they'd always dreamed of throwing for their little girl, who was not a little girl at all, he thought with a smile. Carling was most definitely a woman, and in a short while she would be his wife just as he'd wanted.

It didn't surprise him that he was about to realize his goal. He always managed to succeed in whatever he set out to achieve or acquire.

He remembered the first time he'd become aware of Carling Templeton. His younger sister Holly had shown him a pictorial coverage of a society party in one of the Texas monthly magazines. While Holly admired the glamorous designer dresses worn by the ever-fashionable belles, Kane found his attention riveted by one beautiful young woman in particular.

The caption under the photograph identified her as Carling Templeton, the senator's daughter.

Over the next few months, he found himself scanning sections of local magazines and newspapers he'd never bothered with before. Carling's photographic appearances were frequent, but it took him a while to admit that for some inexplicable, unfathomable reason, the senator's daughter—who was probably an airheaded party girl—intrigued him.

He'd been a longtime contributor to Clayton Templeton's campaign war chest and regularly received invitations to various political fund-raisers and constituency meetings. He finally decided to attend one featuring an appearance by the senator's wife and daughter. It was time to find out if Carling was a shallow little idiot or the woman he wanted her to be....

The question was resoundingly answered on their first meeting. From that moment, Kane wanted Carling. His blood heated at the mere thought of her. She stirred his imagination as no other woman ever had. So he'd bided his time, waiting and watching, dropping hints, both broad and subtle, to her father.

Finally, it had all come together. As an astute business-man with faultless instincts, he had hardly believed the poor judgment and impulsive greed that had sent a desperate, disconsolate Senator Templeton to him. He'd seen his chance and taken it. Kane knew all about opportunity knocking and when and how to respond.

He also knew his own worth, but was under no illusions about his charm—or the lack of it. He was hardworking, outspoken and set in his ways; he preferred to lead a quiet life with few intrusions and little socializing. He knew he lacked the flair of a party-loving extrovert, and could have never wooed and won Carling Templeton in traditional, so-cial fashion.

Then he'd noticed that no other man in her exalted cir-cles seemed capable of wooing and winning her, either. She dated the most eligible young bachelors that Washington, Houston and Dallas had to offer and invariably the rela-tionships went nowhere.

The first time he had observed her, he understood why. She was friendly but reserved, classy and cool, intelligent and charming, the ideal date for those exclusive parties, benefit balls and other elite social functions she was forever attending. But missing were any of those nuances that a sexually eligible and interested woman sends to a potential lover. She was strictly look-but-don't-touch, all polite, charming talk but absolutely no physical action.

"Carling Templeton is an icicle," he'd overheard one disgruntled charm-boy tell another. "Ask anyone and they'll tell you. She's so cold she could freeze liquid nitrogen."

Had anyone asked him, Kane would have disagreed. Carling played it cool—okay, icy, he conceded—but the chemistry arcing between them on their first meeting was as explosive as magnesium to a flame. And that was very explosive indeed, as he remembered from a botched experiment in chem lab. Adding to that was the way she had responded to him today when he'd taken her into his arms. The heat they'd generated was the embodiment of every fantasy he'd ever had about her.

Oh yes, Kane told himself with characteristic infallible conviction; this marriage was going to work out very well indeed.

"Kane?" Neva's voice intruded upon his reverie, jarring him out of it. "Could we possibly prevail upon you to set a wedding date several months from today? Though Carling might not have told you, I know how very much she would love to have the big wedding of her dreams. She used to absolutely adore playing wedding with her paper dolls when she was small. I bought her hundreds of those bride-and-groom sets and she would carefully cut out every single—"

"Mama, I'm sure Kane isn't interested in hearing about my paper doll games." Carling rejoined them in the hall, wearing a tailored beige jacket and matching pencil-slim skirt. She'd switched to a pair of teal blue leather shoes, the shade perfectly matching her blouse, the three-inch heels high and slender, bolstering her height to an impressive five foot nine. Still, she felt dwarfed by Kane's towering frame.

She had also recombed her hair, pulling it into a sleek, smooth chignon without a single strand out of place. She'd fixed her makeup, too, obliterating all traces of that deep, hot kiss they'd shared...

No, she quickly amended—that he'd *forced* upon her.

"Carling, dear, I was just explaining to Kane how we would adore having a wonderful old-fashioned wedding," Neva said eagerly. "Perhaps you two could talk it over and—"

"The thought of a great big society wedding makes my blood run cold," Kane said bluntly. "I can't think of anything I'd hate more."

There was a long moment of silence which wasn't broken until Senator Templeton cleared his throat to speak. "Neva, if Kane and Carling have made up their minds to have a quiet, private wedding, we have to respect their decision.''

"Thanks for your support, Senator. I appreciate it,'' said Kane dryly.

A million nasty, caustic rejoinders leaped to mind, but Carling refrained from uttering any one of them. What was the point? Even if Kane had suggested getting married in a new-age ceremony deep in the bowels of some damp creepy bat cave, her father would have supported him.

"You two are welcome to come along and be our witnesses,'' suggested Kane. "Afterward, we'll have a celebration dinner at Washington's best restaurant, my treat. Just name the place and I'll phone for reservations right now.''

"No, no, you two run along,'' Neva interjected quickly. "Clayton is right. If you want a private wedding, you should have it. And instead of going to a restaurant, why don't you come back to the house afterward? I'll have the cook prepare a special wedding dinner for us here—so much more celebratory and festive than merely dining out.''

Neva shepherded them toward the door as she talked, while the senator stood in the background, staring silently at the floor. Within moments, Carling and Kane were standing outside on the small brick stoop, the front door closed firmly behind them.

"I can see that we come from two different worlds,'' Kane remarked dryly. "In my family, dining out is considered celebratory and festive—eating dinner at home is the everyday routine.''

"That is only one of the minor differences between us. There are several million *major* differences as well,'' snapped Carling. "Which is why the idea of us getting married is not only absurd but sure to be calamitous.''

"We're more alike than you realize. The fact that you agreed to marry me proves it.''

"I didn't agree, I had no choice, so it proves nothing at all!'' She shrugged off his hand when he placed it on her elbow to lead her to his rental car parked in front of the house.

"Doesn't it bother you to know that you're being married strictly for your money?" she demanded. The urge to provoke him, to goad him, was irresistible. "I thought rich men wanted to be married for themselves, not for their fortunes. But not you! What kind of—of weird misfit are you, anyway?"

"The kind of weird misfit who's about to become your husband," he replied complacently.

"That's it! I've had all I can take!" Carling shrieked, her eyes darkening with rage. Abandoning all attempts to stay cool, giving into the ferocious anger pulsing through her, she drew back her hand and slapped him hard across the cheek.

Three

The sound seemed to reverberate around them. Kane laid his fingers to his stinging cheek. "That hurt, Carly," he said coolly. "But you meant it to, of course. Now are you ready to pay the price?"

His other hand snaked out to seize her wrist. Slowly, deliberately, he started to pull her toward him.

She held herself rigid, trying to hold back, but once again his greater strength overcame her resistance. Against her will, she found herself inching toward him.

"You were asking for it! You deserved it and worse!" She sounded fierce, but her anger had been momentarily displaced by pure shock—with herself. "I've never slapped anyone before in my entire life. I happen to be a firm believer in nonviolence, but you forced me into it!"

"Let me get this straight—it's my own fault I got hit? I *made* you do it?"

"Yes!" She tried to jerk her wrist from his steely grip.

"You subscribe to the blame-the-victim school of thought, I see." One final tug brought her up against him. "Let's settle this issue once and for all, Carly. I don't believe in domestic violence and I sure as hell don't believe in letting my future wife haul off and belt me. I want an apology."

"I'm not sorry!" Oh, but she was. Not only for having hit him, but also for the consequences her rash action had provoked. The way he towered over her made her instinctively want to retreat. She frantically tried to take a step back, to put some much-needed distance between them, but it was too late. He had already wrapped his hard, muscular arms around her, firmly anchoring her against him.

"Go on and fight me, baby," he taunted huskily. "You know you want to."

"I do not! I'm hardly the fighting, spitting, scratching she-cat type, Mr. McClellan. If that's what you're looking for in a wife, I suggest you continue your search."

She drew her head back a little and looked up at him. He was so tall and so powerful, simply being near him made her feel vulnerable, and the sensation was intensified when she was in his arms. An alarming weakness began to spread through her, making her feel small and soft and....

"My search for a wife has ended, Carly," he drawled. "When you go to bed tonight, you'll be Mrs. Kane Mc-Clellan."

Her mouth went dry. A vivid image of herself lying nervous and naked, waiting for Kane McClellan to come to her, flashed across her mind. "I believe I should warn you that I'm as cold in bed as out of it." She tried for her most forbidding tone of voice, one that had never failed to discourage even the most audacious suitor. "Hardly an enticing bridal prospect for a—a hotheaded savage like yourself."

Kane was not discouraged. Far from it. "You've honed that prim icicle act of yours to such perfection that even you're beginning to believe it. But I don't buy it, Carly."

He settled her intimately against his big frame. For one heart-stopping moment, the soft mound of her femininity pressed against his erection. Carling gasped at the sharp, dizzying sensation piercing her.

"Under that glacial veneer is a little wildcat," Kane murmured softly, seductively. But he didn't release her; she remained a captive in his arms, the soft, warm curves of her body fitted against and into the sturdy masculine planes of his.

"Let go of me!" she cried, fighting the syrupy warmth stealing through her. That was the only struggle she could hope to win. She'd already learned that it was useless to pit her physical strength against his. She remembered only too well how she'd fought him in the hall earlier, how he'd effortlessly held her and kissed her. Those same hot ripples of pleasure she'd experienced then were building within her again.

He was holding her against her will, but he wasn't hurting her, and it horrified her that some dark primitive part of her was actually responding to his caveman tactics.

"If you don't let me go this minute, one of the neighbors will undoubtedly call the police!" she threatened. The need to lash out at him warred against the urge to melt into him—and won.

"They will?" He sounded genuinely curious. "Why?"

"Because you're molesting me in full public view!"

Kane laughed so hard that he let her go. "Molesting you?" Then he howled all over again.

"It's not funny!" Scowling, Carling quickly moved away from him. "I'm sure that in the isolated wastelands of your ranch your barbaric uncouth behavior goes unnoticed, but may I remind you that we happen to be in a civilized neighborhood where—"

"A man on his way to his wedding is not allowed to touch his fiancée?" Kane suggested helpfully. "Somehow I think that's permissible, even in the most proper neighborhoods."

"Dammit, what do I have to do, what do I have to say to make you take me seriously?" she practically shouted, her cheeks flushed with fury and frustration—and arousal.

"I do take you seriously, sweetheart. What could be more serious than marriage?" He opened the front door of the car, on the passenger side. "Get into the car, Carly. We're leaving."

"I didn't apologize for hitting you," she reminded him quickly. She was stalling for time, grasping at straws. The marriage mill awaited; once she'd gotten into the car with him, she would be doomed.

"You will, eventually." He glanced at his watch. "Carly, if you don't get into the car, I'm afraid I'll have to put you in myself, right in full view of your scandal-mongering neighbors."

It took her less than a second to decide. Tilting her chin regally, she climbed into the car, pausing only to shoot him a smoldering look of dislike. He couldn't have realized how effective his threat about the neighbors actually would be. The proliferation of newspaper and television tabloids had created a wide-open market for those wanting to cash in on scenes and scandals. Someone would be only too happy to report—or film with their home video camera?—Senator Templeton's socialite daughter brawling with a Neanderthal cowboy in front of the Templeton home.

It galled her that she had to obey him but she did, deriving some small satisfaction by sitting as far away from him as the front seat would allow. They drove in silence, Kane weaving in and out of the dense, early-afternoon traffic with an expertise that not even Carling could fault.

"Your father gave me directions to this place when he called me last night," he said. As a conversational sally, it fell flat. Carling stared in icy silence, her lips compressed tightly.

He fiddled with the radio, looking for a station and then asked her to suggest her favorite. She snapped that she didn't listen to the radio in the car. While driving, she preferred to play her foreign language tapes. Thanks to them, she was fluent in Spanish, did passably well with French and was currently learning conversational Japanese.

He shrugged and found a country-western station.

"Your favorite type of music, I presume?" she remarked caustically after a forlorn ballad about loneliness, fast nights and faithless women ended with a guitar-strumming finale.

"You presume correctly," he said. His smile was clearly a peace offering.

One she did not accept. "That figures. It's the only type of music that I absolutely can't abide."

Kane turned the volume higher and the sound of banjos filled the car. "I gave you first choice, honey. Now you're stuck with my choice. A little lesson for the future, maybe?"

"I don't take lessons from you!"

"How about some advice then? I'm more than willing to meet you halfway, but if you're determined to challenge me at every turn, I won't back down or back away. And, baby, you'll end up losing every time."

"That's what you think, you insufferable, arrogant macho clod! If you insist on marrying me, *you'll* be the one in need of lessons and advice. Because *I* do not lose and I'm not about to start now."

"You never lose?" He pretended to ponder that. "I guess it would be insufferable, arrogant and macho of me to point out that you once swore never to have anything to do with me, yet now you're on your way to our wedding."

He paused and reached for her hand, tucking it to rest beneath his hand on his thigh. Because she was sitting so far away from him, her arm was completely outstretched. It was uncomfortable and looked foolish, she knew, but she refused to move closer.

"I'm glad you consider our wedding your own personal victory, sweetheart," Kane continued silkily. "I feel the same. You see how alike we are? A perfect match."

His smooth tone didn't fool her for a minute. He was deliberately baiting her! Carling felt the rough denim of his jeans against her palm, felt the rock-hard muscle of his thigh beneath the cloth. His big hand was covering hers, engulfing it, his fingers lightly stroking hers.

A bolt of electricity rocked her. How could he manage to antagonize and arouse her at the same time? Confusion and rage ripped through her, short-circuiting her emotions. She felt like laughing and crying. Never had she met anyone who could rattle her this way. Everything he did, everything he said, got under her skin and provoked a wild reaction. In fact, he didn't even have to do or say a thing, she acknowledged grimly. His mere presence unsettled and unnerved her.

Glaring balefully at him, she jerked her hand away, rubbing the aching muscles of her arm with her other hand.

Kane appeared to be unaware of her turmoil. "I'm a bit surprised that your parents didn't come with us," he remarked as they passed the road signs welcoming them to the state of Virginia. "It's all or nothing with them, hmm? If their only daughter's wedding isn't a newsworthy super-spectacular, they can't be bothered to attend the ceremony."

"Don't you dare criticize my parents!"

"I wasn't criticizing—well, yes, maybe I was. Still, I admire your loyalty to them, no matter what."

"My parents deserve my love and loyalty and they'll always have it."

"Very admirable," Kane said, nodding his approval. "I understand and appreciate your support for your parents. You have a strong sense of family, Carly. It's a value I share, and shared values are a prerequisite to a successful marriage. That's one of the reasons why I know we're well matched."

"*You* have a family? Reptiles don't, as a rule, you know. I assumed you were hatched before you crawled out from under your rock, like the rest of your species."

He said nothing, irritating her further. She glanced at him covertly. He appeared to be concentrating completely on the roadway. Two of his fingers were lightly tapping the steering wheel, keeping time with the beat of the song blasting from the radio.

For some unfathomable reason, which Carling didn't even try to comprehend, she couldn't stand being ignored by him. Fighting with him was far more preferable. If being likened to a reptile didn't bother him, then perhaps an attack on his family would draw some blood?

"You have the nerve to condemn *my* parents for not coming to this—this farce of a wedding ceremony of ours," she began, her blue eyes alight with a combative glitter. "Well, where are *your* parents? I certainly don't see any evidence of this great family love and loyalty you're boasting about."

"My parents are dead," Kane said flatly.

Carling closed her eyes and suppressed a groan. Her social blunders were few and far between and rarely of this magnitude. "I didn't know," she mumbled. She was so mortified that her hostility was temporarily replaced by her horrified embarrassment.

"I'm terribly sorry." The words came easily, almost automatically. Because over the years she had accompanied her father to countless viewings and funerals of his assorted constituents and colleagues, it was natural for her to slip into that mode.

"Are you?" Kane challenged. "Since you didn't know my folks and you profess to hate me, why should you be sorry?"

She'd never had her perfunctory proclamation of sympathy questioned before. Carling was flustered. "Well, because—I—of course, I didn't know them but I'm sorry—that is, I'm certainly not glad to hear that they—uh—passed away."

Her face flamed. A practiced, smooth public speaker, she'd never made such a mangled mess of a remark in her life. She was determined to make amends and regain her composure. "How— When did you lose your parents, Kane?"

"They're not lost, they're dead," he said bluntly. "I know you probably mean well, but I detest euphemisms."

She swallowed. "I grew up speaking in euphemisms. It's practically the official language of politics."

"How true. Just this morning I heard two congressmen on the radio, debating the pros and cons of 'negative tax reduction' and 'revenue enhancement.'"

"Two of the more creative terms used in order to avoid that dreaded, guaranteed election-loser known as raising taxes," she admitted sheepishly.

The quick, droll smile he gave her made her feel a warm thrust deep in her abdomen. Carling forgot to exhale. When her body demanded that she begin breathing again, she had to gulp for air. She was in deep, deep trouble and she knew it. When his smile affected her so profoundly...when his touch made her burn with a restlessness she had never previously experienced...

Carling tensed. She couldn't be softening toward him! The thought was too appalling to imagine. She shook her head, as if to shake off the idea. She would not, could not, be seduced by this arrogant, infuriating man.

He was *buying* her, Carling reminded herself bitterly. He'd written a check to obtain her, as if he were paying for a bag of groceries at a supermarket. A helpless rage streaked through her. Being his bought-and-paid-for-bride would certainly mean the loss of her freedom and independence. A domineering man like Kane McClellan would settle for nothing less than total subservience to him.

He was forcing her to give up everything that was important to her, her home and friends and social activities, to lead a life of reclusive desolation on his wretched ranch deep in the middle of no-man's-land. But he couldn't force her to like him or care for him or want him, she reassured herself. He was her enemy and she wasn't about to forget it. And oh, would she make him sorry that he had purchased her so cold-bloodedly!

"You asked how and when my folks died," Kane said, breaking into her vengeful fantasies and successfully disconcerting her once again. "They were killed in a car accident twelve years ago, a week after my twenty-third birthday. One of my younger brothers was with them and was critically injured. He died ten days later."

She wasn't so cold-hearted that she could be indifferent to such a monumental tragedy, even if he was her avowed enemy. Carling temporarily shelved her diabolical fantasies of how to make his life unendurable. "It must have been terrible," she said quietly. "I can't imagine losing my parents. And to lose your brother, too..."

Her voice trailed off. It was too awful to contemplate, let alone put into words. Her all-purpose "I'm sorry" just didn't cover the enormity of it.

"It was tough."

She saw him tighten his grip on the steering wheel and somehow understood the volume of emotion behind those three simple words. "What happened?"

"They were driving my brother John back to college when they were hit head-on by a drunk driver going the wrong way on the interstate. John was twenty-one and a senior at Rice University. My old alma mater," he added with a slight smile.

"You graduated from Rice?" That was a surprise. She thought he'd never ventured from the old homestead.

Kane nodded. "I went on to the Wharton School of Business after graduation. I'd planned to become an investment banker—you know, live in New York, make a pile of money. I was just finishing up my MBA at the time of the accident."

Her eyes slid over him. From the moment she'd first seen him, she had thought he looked the part of the quintessential cowboy. This new information caused her preconceptions to shift as she tried to picture him in a custom-tailored suit, sitting behind a desk in a Wall Street office.

She simply couldn't. He looked like a man who worked outdoors, one who could chop a cord of wood in his spare time and not even get winded. A citified, desk-bound Kane McClellan was beyond her ken. "You—obviously didn't go to New York," she ventured a guess.

"No. I went home immediately. In addition to the ranch, there were the other kids—my two little brothers and my baby sister. There was a big age gap between the three of them and John and me. Our mother had had several miscarriages during those years and had given up hope of having any more kids. Then Scott finally arrived when I was eleven. Holly was born two years later and then Tim just a year after that."

"So they were very young when your parents were killed." Carling did some quick mental arithmetic. "Twelve, ten and nine. How sad for those poor children!"

"I was named their legal guardian and returned to the ranch to raise them. They're all grown up now. And doing well, too." He flashed a proud, fraternal smile. "Tim is a brilliant student at Rice. He's a senior this year and has already been accepted into medical school. Last year Holly graduated from a women's college in Atlanta and is currently living at the ranch, learning the ropes. I think she has her heart set on becoming a rancher's wife, and nothing could please me more," he added with satisfaction.

"She's very young. Does she want to get married?" Carling asked coolly. "Or are you arranging a marriage for her in your inimitable feudal fashion?"

He ignored the jibe. "The Waynes, our nearest neighbors, have a son, Joseph, who's Holly's age, and the two of them have been seeing a lot of each other since Holly returned home. They don't need me to arrange things for them. As for Scott, he majored in partying at the University in Austin, but after six years finally managed to graduate and, thankfully, seems to have settled down. He's now a bank management trainee in Dallas."

"It sounds as if you did a good job raising them," Carling said with grudging admiration. It couldn't have been easy for a young man in his early twenties to take sole responsibility for three children, along with having to cope with the terrible grief of losing the other half of his family.

But somehow it didn't surprise her that Kane McClellan had successfully done so. She was already learning that he was the kind of person who achieved what he set out to do. And then she was struck by a ghastly insight: since Kane had been forced by fate to give up his plans and change his life, he probably had no compunction about expecting her to do the same!

He would never understand the magnitude of her loss of freedom. Hadn't he accepted and adjusted in a similar situation? No wonder he fully expected her to settle down to domestic life on that godforsaken ranch without regret or a backward glance—he had done the same thing.

"There were some rough times, though, particularly when the kids were teenagers," Kane admitted. "Tim was always easygoing and dependable, a pleasure to have around, but Scott and Holly each went through a rebellious period. Fortunately, that's all behind us."

"What do they think about your crazy idea of marrying a woman you hardly know and they don't know at all?" she demanded. The brief frown that crossed his face was all the answer she needed. "They don't know!" she accused. "You didn't tell them you were getting married. You're planning to spring me on them—"

"I don't have to clear my actions with the kids. They—"

"But I bet *they* have to clear their actions with *you*," Carling interrupted snidely. "You wouldn't have it any other way. Growing up with you in charge must've been like living in a totalitarian regime."

"The kids and I get along very well," Kane insisted. "In fact, seeing how well the three of them turned out has given me the confidence and inspiration to raise children of my own."

Carling froze. This was where she came into the picture. "I don't know very much about children," she said swiftly. "I'm an only child with no cousins near my age and I never had baby-sitting jobs when I was a teenager."

"You'll be a fine mother," Kane said soothingly. "Maternal instinct goes a long way and there are plenty of books and videos on child care to fill in the gaps. Besides, I'll be right there to help you. I intend to be a very involved father, not an absent one."

"I'm not worried about what kind of mother I'll be," Carling gritted out through clenched teeth. "But when I have children, I want it to be my choice and with the man of my choice."

"He's sitting right beside you, sweetheart. You just haven't realized it yet. But you will. As for when to have kids, for us it's the sooner the better. Our biological clocks are ticking away."

"I have quite a few years before the alarm goes off!" she protested indignantly.

"You may not have had much experience with children, but you like them," he continued, his voice smooth and sure. "You enjoy your friends' and neighbors' children. You want a baby of your own—in fact, several of them. You don't want to raise an only child because you were often lonely growing up."

He was repeating comments she'd made in public over the years, and they were all true. But hearing him use her own words to bolster *his* position was like being shot down with her own ammunition. "Don't quote me to myself!" she snapped.

He merely smiled. "You'll be a conscientious full-time mother, who can devote herself completely to her family without the demands and hassles of an outside career interfering with your primary responsibilities."

Uh-oh! Carling gulped. She recognized that statement. She'd said it often enough to the various conservative groups, which were the foundation of her father's political strength. She tried to come up with an effective rebuttal, but nothing came to mind. When she opened her mouth to speak, there were no words to be said.

"No comment?" Kane asked mildly.

Carling clenched her fists. He had her there, and he knew it! Though his expression was calm and implacable, she was absolutely certain that he was silently, triumphantly laughing at her.

"I should've guessed that a sexist pig like you wouldn't approve of—of career women!" She had to admit to herself it was a rather weak salvo coming from her, the senator's daughter, who regularly took potshots at career women because they were easy targets in the domestic arena of the political battlefield. If Kane were any kind of a gentleman, he would let it pass and not call her on it.

Naturally, that didn't happen and call her on it he did. "Lame, Carly." This time he didn't bother to conceal his laughter. "You and your daddy and his crowd are the ones who lambaste women who choose careers instead of total domesticity, not me. I happen to respect them. That's why I would never ask a woman who has invested years of her life in studying for a profession, who has built a successful career, to leave it all to become a full-time wife and mother on my ranch. It wouldn't be fair to her."

"You mean if I were a doctor or lawyer or teacher or something, you wouldn't—wouldn't—"

"Be interested in marrying you? That's correct, I wouldn't. Because I'd know you would be unhappy, far from the city and your profession, and I don't want an unhappy wife. I told you I'd researched this very seriously, Carly. You were raised to be a wife and mother. You believe a woman is happiest devoting herself to raising a family. And that's exactly what you're going to spend the rest of your life doing. With me."

She couldn't speak, she couldn't breathe. For one wild moment, she wondered if he were an agent for one of those opposition groups her father and his allies were always at war with, an enemy whose assignment it was to make her live the words she so glibly espoused.

She was trapped, and the hopelessness of her situation struck her with renewed force. "Oh, what's the use in trying to reason with you? Talking to you is like talking to a brick wall." How she wished she could come up with something more original, but she was too overwrought to be clever. He had already bested her at every turn.

"So I've been told," Kane agreed with maddening good humor. "Relax, Carly, everything is going to work out fine. Do you really think I would marry you if I thought there was a chance that it wouldn't?"

"I have no faith in your judgment. I think you're insane! Who else but a crazy man would insist on marrying a—a woman who hates him, who is determined to make his life a misery beyond anyone's wildest imagination!"

"Is that what you're planning, Carly? To make my life miserable?" He sounded amused.

"Oh yes," she vowed with heartfelt vehemence. "I guarantee that you'll find living with me so intolerable, you'll soon be begging me to go."

"And I guarantee that won't happen," he replied with equal intensity. "Loyalty is an intrinsic part of your character, Carly. This marriage of ours proves how loyal a daughter you really are. It goes without saying that you will be loyal and loving to your husband, and to your children as well. Anyway, if you were to be honest with yourself, you'd admit that it's time for a change in your life. You weren't happy with things the way they were. The party-social circuit was beginning to pall for you," he added with a certainty that took her breath away.

"You've said a lot of outrageously arrogant things today, but you—you've outdone yourself with that one," she spluttered furiously. "I was thoroughly enjoying my life exactly the way I was living it. For you to say otherwise is to—"

"State the facts," he finished calmly. "I happen to know them, honey. Your father has been hounding you unmercifully to hook up with a husband with enough money to keep the Templetons in the style to which they've become accustomed. So you went through the motions of looking for Mr. Rich. You dated Quentin Ramsey's boy, Jed, and Cole Tremaine, to name only your most recent candidates."

"Who are you? A member of some spy network? How do you know so much about my personal life?"

"Meticulous research. I used the same approach in choosing a wife that I do in my investments, Carly. There is little—if anything—about you that I don't know."

"Is that so?" She glared at him. No woman could listen to a man make such a smug, doggedly confident statement about her without feeling homicidal. Unfortunately, she would have to limit herself to verbally annihilating him.

"Yes. And I noticed an interesting pattern in your behavior. You seemed to have an uncanny knack of finding ways to keep the men you were supposedly considering as matrimonial prospects from considering *you* as one."

She'd been mulling over the most insulting, vicious thing she could possibly say to him, but he threw her completely off balance with that observation. It was disturbingly close to the mark, and of course, she denied it. "I don't know what you're talking about, but it doesn't matter because nothing you say interests me anyway."

He laughed. "You no more wanted to marry Jed Ramsey than you wanted to hike barefoot across the desert, but you pressured him, let him think that you and your father were cooking up a conspiracy with his father to drag him to the altar. Naturally, poor Jed took off—what self-respecting bachelor wouldn't? And you were saved from your father's expectations because Ramsey married another woman not very long afterward."

She folded her arms across her chest and stared stonily ahead, pretending that she wasn't listening to him. But she was.

"And then there was Cole Tremaine," Kane continued. "Infinitely eligible, everything your father wanted in a husband for you. Wealthy, handsome, successful, from a good family. But did you even try to make him see you as a desirable, sexually eligible woman? No, you played it strictly as friends. A sexless, platonic, this-relationship-will-go-nowhere friendship. It came as no surprise when he married another woman, except to your poor, desperate father."

"And now look who I'm stuck with!" she burst out. "Anyone else I've ever dated would have been infinitely preferable to *you!*"

"Because I turn you on like no other man ever has and you don't know how to handle it?"

"Because you're the most conceited, revolting chauvinistic tyrant I've ever met!"

"That's not it at all. You can't help responding to me and you're scared to death of losing that icy control you've encased yourself in. But you're going to lose it. The barriers come down tonight."

"No!"

"Oh yes, sweet Carly." His grin was positively wicked.

"I won't even dignify that with a reply," she sniffed with a grand, self-righteous air.

"We're here," Kane announced a short time later, as he braked to a stop in a wide parking lot adjacent to a tall office building.

They walked inside, his hand resting on the small of her back in a proprietary fashion. This must be the way a condemned prisoner feels on his way to meet the firing squad, Carling thought bleakly. Hopeless, helpless, with all appeals for a reprieve denied.

A kind of merciful numbness set in, and as if in a trance, she went through the motions of filling out forms, getting a blood test and waiting the requisite few hours for a marriage license. Kane stayed at her side, alternately talkative

and silent, frequently touching her, watching her, his gray
eyes intense and blatantly sensual.

Finally, they were ushered before the judge who pro-
nounced them man and wife and then wished them well.
Carling stared down at the thick gold wedding band on the
third finger of her left hand, the ring that Kane had placed
there. Because she couldn't take her eyes off it, she was surprised when Kane cupped her chin with his big hand and
tilted it upward.

Their eyes met. "Isn't this the part where the groom tra-
ditionally kisses his bride?" he asked softly.

He lowered his head and lightly pressed his mouth to hers.

She was too startled, too dazed to react the way she would
have, had she not been so off balance. His lips were warm
and full on hers, gentle and unthreatening. Her eyelids felt
oddly heavy and dropped shut. He seductively increased the
pressure as his mouth opened over hers and unconsciously,
instinctively, she put her hand on his chest.

She could feel his solid, muscular strength and the steady
thudding of his heart beneath her palm. When his tongue
slipped into her mouth and massaged hers, a twinge of pure
physical desire pierced her deeply.

Her eyes flew open at the same moment that he lifted his
lips from hers. She was aware that her face was flushed and
that her breathing had quickened. It was no use denying it,
not even to herself: for one fleeting moment she had been
oblivious of their surroundings, to the dull, institutional
setting of the judge's office, even to the judge himself.

"Ready to go, Mrs. McClellan?" Kane asked huskily,
taking her hand in his. "The sooner we get the celebration
dinner with your parents over with, the sooner we can be
alone together."

Carling made a strangled, incoherent reply. An aura of
unreality enveloped her. This couldn't be happening! She
was staring at the wedding ring again and the sound of "Mrs
McClellan" was ringing in her ears. Mrs. McClellan—that
was her!

She was married. Married! And to the one man she knew she could never control, could never keep at a distance, the one man who would never be content to let her go blithely on her way while he went his. She glanced wildly at him.

"This can't be happening," she whispered, vocalizing her thoughts.

"I made hotel reservations for tonight at a place near the airport," Kane kept talking as he walked her out of the room, out of the building, and back toward the car. "My plane is being serviced there and we'll fly out in the morning."

She couldn't let herself think about the two of them in a hotel room tonight. "Your plane?" she asked in an attempt to divert herself and him. Her throat was dry and her voice squeaked.

"It's a twin engine Cessna 310. Since I have a pilot's license, I flew it up myself. The ranch has its own small airstrip, so we'll be able to fly directly there tomorrow."

He had his own plane; his ranch had its own airstrip. He had been able to come up with a huge amount of money almost immediately and didn't look for repayment of the loan. For the first time, Carling realized just how wealthy Kane McClellan really was.

He was rich enough to buy the woman he professed to want for his wife, to marry her against her will. Rich enough to keep her for as long as he chose. Rich, strong and powerful enough to make her do whatever he wanted. It was a chilling observation and Carling shivered, despite the warm April sunshine.

The drive back to her parents' house was smooth and swift. Kane played the country-western station, sometimes whistling along with the music. Carling folded her hands tightly in her lap and rode in shaken silence. She couldn't waste her energy fighting with him, not now. She had to conserve every bit of her strength and her wits for tonight when she would successfully outsmart and outmaneuver her captor—her husband, Kane McClellan.

Four

Carling immediately recognized the caterer's van parked in her parents' driveway. *Capitol Affairs* was her mother's favorite catering service.

Kane read the logo printed on the van as he pulled up behind it. "So much for a home-cooked meal," he said, groaning. "I'd rather have gone to a restaurant than face this. Every catered meal I've ever eaten has tasted like warmed-over airline food."

"The food that *Capitol Affairs* serves has always been uniformly excellent," Carling retorted loyally. "They're the most popular catering service in the District."

"That's not saying a whole lot, especially since they're free to run over here on a moment's notice with their supply of edible plastics."

"It's a tribute to my mother that they're here on such short notice for a small simple family dinner..." Her voice trailed off. She'd just noticed all the cars lining the street, parked along both sides for as far as she could see. "Which might not be so small and simple after all."

Kane followed her gaze. "You don't think—" he began warily.

"That my mother has managed to throw together a party for us? That's exactly what I think."

"After I specifically said I didn't want a big society wedding?" Kane was frowning, clearly displeased.

His obvious displeasure, his disapproval, buoyed Carling's flagging spirits immensely. "We didn't have one," she reminded him. "And you made no objections to a large society reception afterwards."

"That's because it didn't occur to me to object. It didn't seem necessary. Who would ever suspect that anyone could put together an affair of this size in just a few hours?"

"That shows how little you know about Neva Templeton," Carling replied with a wry smile. "I should've known Mother was up to something—she gave up on the big wedding idea far too easily. No wonder she was so eager to get us out of the house. She must've started making phone calls before we were even in the car."

"Surely all those cars can't belong to your parents' guests?" Kane squinted at the seemingly endless lines of cars and scowled ferociously.

This was not at all what he had had in mind. He had considered even a quiet dinner with Carling's parents an intrusion, but he'd accepted it as a necessary obligation before commencing their wedding night.

"Unbelievable," he growled. "I hate big parties even when I know and like all the guests. Now I'm supposed to tolerate this extravaganza full of strangers?"

"They're not strangers to my family," countered Carling.

"Right. They're your thousands upon thousands of *close friends*."

"Well, since you insisted upon marrying a stranger, you might as well party with strangers, too."

He arched his eyebrows. "You're enjoying this, aren't you?" he drawled. "You didn't even try to keep the malicious glee out of your voice."

"If you're uncomfortable, unhappy or uneasy in any way, I'm thrilled. Although the idea of parading in there as Mrs. Kane McClellan is enough to make me break out in hives."

"Do you want to skip it and go directly to the hotel instead?" His smile was wolfish, his eyes challenging. As usual, he had completely ignored the insult, thereby putting her back on the defensive.

"No!" Carling hated the panic in her voice and hated Kane for putting it there. "I'd rather face any crowd, no matter how big or how curious, than be alone with *you!*"

Flinging open the car door, she rushed immediately toward the front door of the house. But by the time she'd reached it, Kane was already at her side, his long strides having easily closed the distance between them. He took her hand, interlacing his fingers with hers.

"Don't you want to present a united front to our well-wishers? We're supposed to be so wildly in love that we impulsively eloped, remember?"

Carling burned. That amused, slightly taunting tone of his was capable of driving her to mayhem. She, cool-as-ice Carling, never felt cool around him for very long, she admitted to herself. And instead of ignoring him with icy silence—her usual method of punishing those who angered her—she wanted to do something alarmingly physical to him.

Something like wiping that confident little smile off his face with the palm of her hand. Her mind conjured up another tantalizingly vicious possibility. She would give him a push with both her hands so that he lost his balance and fell to the ground; next, she would—

And then she felt his thumb begin to move over her palm, stroking in a slow suggestive rhythm, back and forth, up and down and around. The pad of his thumb was callused, abrasive against her soft, sensitive skin.

The caress affected her like an electric current, exploding in hot sparks in the deep, secret place between her legs. Carling drew in a sharp breath. The volatile pleasure made her head spin, and to her great shame she didn't gasp in outrage and jerk her hand away instantaneously. It wasn't until he lifted her hand to his mouth and pressed his lips against the palm he'd sensitized with his caress that a stunned Carling managed to summon enough willpower for the requisite gasping withdrawal.

"Don't!" she ordered in a voice far, far removed from the usual imperious tones she used to dissuade amorous would-be swains. Flushed and trembling, she found it impossible to look at him.

"Don't?" He pretended to be puzzled. "Why not? You liked it."

"I didn't!"

"You loved it, Carly. I was watching you. You were getting aroused from just that simple caress."

"That's purely wishful thinking based on your incredibly oversized ego!"

"It's a fact based on observation. I saw you squirming. You were squeezing your thighs together trying to—"

Carling uttered a strangled cry and pushed open the door. Her mother spotted her at once and proceeded to weave her way swiftly through the crowded vestibule toward her.

"Darling, you're here!" Neva Templeton exclaimed joyfully, throwing her arms around her daughter. "Dixie Lee said that she thought she saw you and your handsome new husband coming up the walk. Oh, and here is that marvelous new son-in-law of mine!"

Carling whirled around to see Kane come up behind her. Neva instantly released her daughter to embrace him. "I can't wait to show you off to all our friends. Such a lovely couple!"

Linking one arm through Carling's and the other through Kane's, Neva purposefully steered them into the large living room, which was crowded to overflowing with guests.

"Here are the bride and groom," she announced to everyone. "Mr. and Mrs. Kane McClellan."

For just a fraction of a second, Kane's and Carling's eyes met. They exchanged mutual pained glances. He truly hated being in the spotlight. And while she usually thoroughly enjoyed being the center of attention, this time was the proverbial exception to the rule.

They were engulfed by swarms of people, and Carling reflexively slipped into her lifelong role as the gregarious, crowd-pleasing daughter of the perennial vote-seeking politician. She smiled and made the appropriate responses to the proffered remarks and remembered everyone's name. Her polished small talk was pleasant.

Kane, not a crowd-pleaser by birth or by choice, didn't even try to match his bride's performance. He stoically endured the endless introductions, but his expression remained serious and unsmiling as men shook his hand or slapped his shoulder, and women leaned up to kiss his cheek or hug him. The displays of faux affection were as disconcerting as the loud, meaningless conversations swirling around him. Did all the women have high-pitched voices that rose to eardrum-shattering decibels as they prattled on? Did all the men boom the guffaws which inevitably followed those spectacularly unfunny jokes?

One voice finally rose above them all—that of Senator Clayton Templeton. "Friends, we have a very special guest with us today and he is going to help us make this truly memorable day an absolutely unforgettable one."

Kane's lips twitched at the redundant hyperbole. The senator's speech writers must not have been available today. He glanced across the room at Carling, who was surrounded by a circle of excited, talkative young women.

"Carling, you sly dog, you!" squealed Marla Madison, who'd known Carling since their debutante days. "I can't believe you've been holding out on us! Keeping that *hunk* all to yourself until you grabbed the gold ring—literally!"

The women shrieked at the pun. Carling winced.

"Smart move, Carling," said Dixie Lee Shaw, the daughter of another southern senator. "The way Marla has been drooling over the guy, she would've definitely posed a threat. You were right to see him on the sly until you nailed him."

"What makes you think I'm no longer a threat?" Marla purred. "Husbands have been known to stray, you know. Kane McClellan would be worth waging an all-out campaign for. He's one of those *real* men that we city girls seldom get to meet. A man who can carry a woman to the bedroom without throwing out his back. A man who wouldn't borrow your mousse and blow-dryer to style his own hair. A man who can down a shot of whisky instead of sipping chilled white wine. A man who—"

"We get the idea, Marla," Debbie Marino, a longtime friend and neighbor of the Templetons, interjected dryly. "And your adultery plot—on Carling's wedding day!—goes beyond tastelessness, even for you."

"It's okay," Carling said hastily. A malevolent smile lit her face. "If Marla wants to make a play for Kane, let her try." What an ingenious solution to her dilemma! Marla was sultry and sexy. If she were to capture Kane's interest . . .

For one brief shining moment, Carling imagined herself gleefully agreeing to hand over her groom to the other woman. And as a condition to regaining his freedom, Kane would hand over the documents containing the records of his financial transactions on Senator Templeton's behalf. Her father would be free from the threat of investigation and she would be free from McClellan and the threat of life on his ramshackle ranch!

Her friends, completely unaware of her fantasy and the real reason behind her sudden marriage, totally misinterpreted her invitation to Marla.

"Carling is so sure that her man is crazy about her that she's challenging Marla to try to come between them!" exclaimed Cookie Loring, a Texas congressman's young second wife. "That's so sweet!"

"Every bride should feel such confidence in her new husband's love," Debbie Marino added warmly.

"Carling, do you plan to start a family right away or are you going to wait a few years?" asked Cookie.

Carling suppressed a groan. She couldn't take much more of this. She was grateful when Kim Hypes, one of her father's junior administrative assistants, joined them.

"Congratulations, Carling," Kim exclaimed with an approving smile. "Your father was beginning to worry that you'd never break out of the luncheon-shopping-party rut, but you did it! I hope you and Kane will be very happy. Of course, I know you will be! What could be more fun than living on a ranch?"

"I can think of at least three things," muttered Marla as Kim left to join another group. "Luncheons, shopping and parties. I'd rather be stuck in that rut than trapped in the wastelands of a Texas ranch."

"But she'll be trapped with a *real man,*" Dixie Lee reminded her.

"True, but she can't spend *all* her time in bed with him," retorted Marla. "Carling, honey, what are you going to do with yourself when your sexy rancher is off roping steers? Will you take up quilting or churning butter or something?"

Carling felt sick. Hearing Marla outline the hellish existence awaiting her made her want to run screaming from the house. Living in isolation on a decrepit ranch, sex with Kane McClellan, quilting, churning...it was too awful to contemplate. What was she going to do?

"Carling, dearest, come on over here!" she heard her father call. "Reverend Wilkes has arrived and is going to perform the wedding ceremony, right here and now."

Reverend Wilkes from their church? *Wedding ceremony?* Carling was dumbfounded. She was pushed through the throng before she had a chance to utter a word. Reverend Wilkes was standing by the front window, holding the Templeton family Bible, an heirloom from three generations past. Kane arrived at the spot at the same time that she did. His face was devoid of expression, but there was a steely glint in his gray eyes.

"Your daddy and I respected your wish to have a very private wedding," Neva Templeton explained to her daughter. "But we couldn't bear not having your union blessed by the word of the Lord. Reverend Wilkes is here to marry the two of you all over again, this time in a religious ceremony."

She raised her eyes pleadingly to Kane. "I hope you don't mind, Kane. Of course, if you have any objections, Reverend Wilkes and the senator and myself will certainly understand."

"Of course I have no objections to a religious ceremony, Neva," said Kane. He glanced down at his bride's mutinous face. "I like the idea of being married twice to my beautiful bride. Makes the marriage seem airtight, hmm?"

That was exactly the way it struck Carling, too. She'd been able to distance herself somewhat from the unfamiliar judge and the brief, legal ceremony, which had been performed at the county building. But to have Reverend Wilkes marry them right here in her own house in front of friends and family, to have to listen to the familiar and meaningful biblical wedding phrases of the wedding ceremony...

A wedding like that combined the emotional with the intellectual, the spiritual with the secular. A wedding like that implied forever.

"Mama, there's really no need to drag Reverent Wilkes *or* the Lord into this," Carling whispered frantically. "I mean, what with—uh—everything going on in the world today, I'm sure they both have other more important things to deal with and—"

"I seem to recall that the Lord likes weddings," Kane put in. "Remember the one at Cana? And from the smile on Reverend Wilkes's face, it's obvious he's glad to be here too."

Neva beamed her approval. Carling shot Kane a black look.

"Reverend Wilkes," Senator Templeton exclaimed heartily. "Let's get on with it!"

"Dearly beloved," intoned the pastor, "we are gathered here today..."

It was adding insult to injury, Carling thought grimly. Rubbing salt into an open wound. Married twice to the same awful man. Forced to endure *two* marriage ceremonies against her will.

After the second ceremony was over, Carling was grateful for the multitude of guests. Their presence kept her away from her husband's side. During much of the boisterous reception, she and Kane McClellan weren't even in the same room—which suited Carling just fine.

It did not suit Kane at all. Ninety minutes of enforced socializing exceeded his tolerance by at least eighty minutes. He glanced at his watch, excused himself from the circle of people who surrounded him and moved purposefully from room to room until he spotted Carling. She was sitting in a corner of the den, engaged in conversation with an attractive young couple who were taking turns passing a fretful baby back and forth between them.

He immediately joined the group, barely glancing at the couple or the dark-haired infant currently being cuddled in its mother's arms. "We're leaving, Carly," he said without preamble.

Carling tried to swallow back the panic, which rose like bile in her throat. She couldn't leave yet. Leaving meant being alone with him and . . . She turned pale, unwilling to let herself consider exactly what that meant.

"Kane, you haven't met the Tremaines," she said quickly, in an effort to delay their departure. "This is Cole, Chelsea, and little Daniel. Daniel isn't having a very good time," she added with a smile at the baby, who was making small sounds of definite displeasure.

"He wants to go home and I'm in complete sympathy with him," Kane said. "I want to leave, too."

Carling winced. "This is my—my husband, Kane McClellan," she told the Tremaines. She watched the couple exchange frankly speculative glances and longed to sink through the floor.

"Cole Tremaine," Kane said thoughtfully. "You dated my wife before you married your own."

"That's true," Cole replied. He studied Kane with unconcealed curiosity. "Chelsea and I were astounded to read about your engagement in the paper today and even more astonished to receive Neva and Clayton's invitation to this party. We weren't aware that you and Carling were even—uh—dating."

Carling stared at the floor in embarrassed silence. She'd used her dates with Cole as a smoke screen in order to divert her father from his matchmaking campaign on behalf of Kane McClellan. Cole had been doing her a favor. There had never been a romance between them, and she'd been quite vocal in expressing to him her loathing for Kane McClellan—along with her determination to never marry the reclusive rancher. It was no wonder that the Tremaines were incredulous.

Incredulous *and* suspicious. Chelsea Tremaine shifted the baby in her arms and stared from Carling to Kane with questioning eyes. "Is everything all right?" Chelsea asked bluntly, the first person of the day to do so, the first one *not* to assume that this marriage was the culmination of a grand romance.

Carling was horrified to feel her eyes suddenly fill with tears and she gulped back the lump that swiftly lodged in her throat. Part of her, the pampered little girl who'd always been catered to and indulged, wanted to give into the tears and beg the Tremaines for help; Cole was a rich and powerful man and he could...

Could what? demanded the other part of her, the adult self, the one who'd taken on responsibility and recognized the irrefutable laws of cause and effect. Cole Tremaine couldn't help her father. She was the only one who could do that. There was no one who could help her.

"Carling, there's no need to pretend with us," Chelsea continued. Apparently, Carling's delay in replying had provided Chelsea with the answer. "If something's wrong, if you're in some kind of trouble, Cole and I will be glad to help you."

Cole nodded in affirmation.

"I'm sure my wife appreciates your loyalty," Kane replied dryly. He looked at Carling, his dark eyebrows arched. "Your friends are concerned about you, honey. Please tell them if there is anything wrong."

Carling held her head a little higher. How dare that snake bait her this way! But however vain or foolish it might be, she simply couldn't bring herself to admit to her well-meaning friends that she'd been literally trapped into marrying Kane McClellan. The Templeton pride, her own as well as her father's, was considerable—and deeply ingrained.

So much so that Carling forced herself to present a passable imitation of a smile and managed to ask gaily, "What could possibly be wrong? It's our wedding day. And we feel quite smug about having kept our—our relationship a secret from everyone. That's a major feat in this town where everybody knows everybody else's business."

Chelsea and Cole stared at her in patent disbelief. Kane was grinning, obviously amused by her performance. Carling longed to clobber him. But she didn't. Keeping up her performance, avoiding Cole's and Chelsea's eyes, she continued brightly, "And we can't leave the party just yet, Kane. It's too early and we're the guests of honor. We haven't even cut the cake yet or—"

"We'll cut the cake now and then you can go upstairs and pack a suitcase or two," Kane interjected. "I'll arrange for the rest of your things to be shipped to the ranch within the week." He nodded to the Tremaines, then placed his arm firmly around Carling's shoulders to lead her away.

"I want to stay. We *owe* it to everybody to stay," she insisted. She had to keep him at bay for at least a few more hours. Maybe by then she'd think up some plan of escape. She had to come up with something, but she needed more time. "My folks went to all the trouble and expense of giving this party for us and all these people cared enough to come and—"

"For the past interminable hour and a half, I've been heartily slapped and smacked. I've been joked with, fawned over, and even flirted with. Whatever I *owe* these good folks has been paid in full. As for the cost of the party, I fully expect your father to forward the bills to me as part of our agreement. So I feel no guilt about leaving while everybody stays and enjoys my hospitality."

Carling stopped short. "What do you mean, you expect Daddy to forward the bills to you as part of your agreement?" she demanded in a hoarse whisper.

"Your father asked me to pay all of your outstanding bills up to and including any incurred on our wedding day. I have no doubt that this party will be considered one of them."

"All my outstanding bills?" she repeated incredulously.

He nodded. "All your credit card bills, your phone bill, your car payments, your personal charge accounts at the local shops."

"No!" Carling felt her cheeks grow hot. She couldn't believe it—she wouldn't! "You're lying. Daddy isn't greedy. He wouldn't bleed you for money in any way and particularly not where I'm concerned."

"I try not to think in terms of greed and bleed, I prefer to take a more positive view," Kane said dryly. "So I looked upon acquiring your debts as a sort of dowry in reverse."

Glumly, she forced herself to face the facts. Kane wasn't lying; he was too frank, too outspoken, too *confident* to resort to that. Never had she felt so demoralized. Not only had her father sanctioned her sale to Kane McClellan, he'd stuck Kane with all her debts!

"I paid off your accounts but there was one bill I was curious about," Kane continued. His gray eyes were gleaming. "The three hundred dollars you charged at a store called *Her Secret*. Her secret what? And why did you need three hundred dollars worth of it?"

"I—I see my mother. I'll tell her about cutting the cake now," Carling said chokingly. She pulled away from him and fairly crashed through the crowd to reach her mother's side. She had to get away from Kane. Her whole body was one scarlet blush, right down to the dusky rose silk teddy she was wearing under her suit. Beautiful, feminine lingerie was her private weakness—and she bought much of it at *Her Secret*, an exclusive lingerie boutique.

But for Kane to know...for him to have paid for the very teddy and sheer silk stockings that she was wearing...Carling was horrified.

The cake cutting was accomplished in record time. Both Kane and Carling resisted the photographer's entreaties to feed each other a piece of wedding cake, an event which was to have been captured for posterity.

"I'm sorry but I simply can't eat a single bite of cake." Carling's voice was shrill with false gaiety. "I've eaten entirely too much of all this wonderful food today." In truth, she hadn't touched a morsel; she was too nervous, her stomach too jumpy.

"I think I'll have dessert later," said Kane.

The jovial crowd found the sexual innuendo in his remark highly amusing and many ribald comments followed. Carling felt as if her smile was permanently plastered onto her face. She found none of the jokes even remotely funny; she vacillated from wanting to rage in fury at the jocular group to wanting to plead with them for help. But she did neither; she just kept on smiling.

"Upstairs," Kane murmured against her ear. "You have twenty minutes to pack and then we're leaving. I've had all the party fun I can handle."

It was a relief to leave the noisy crowd and escape to the quiet solitude of her room. For a few moments, Carling sat on her bed and stared out the window at the darkening sky. The earlier sunshine had been displaced by gray storm clouds, and the dismal gloom outdoors matched her mood. The unthinkable was about to happen, the unbelievable about to become reality. She was going to have to leave her home, her family and friends—to live with Kane Mc-Clellan.

But even that horror paled in comparison with her more immediate fate—going to bed with him tonight. Choking back a cry, Carling jumped up and sprang into action. Anything was better than passively sitting here and thinking about what awaited her. She retrieved her suitcases from a hall storage closet and began to pack.

She didn't stop until three suitcases and two canvas tote bags were stuffed to overflowing. Though the task was completed, she was loath to leave the peacefulness of her room. Carling grimaced as she recalled her mother stopping her on her way up the stairs and asking her if she was going to change into a "going-away outfit".

A "going-away outfit," indeed! What did a bought-and-paid-for slave wear when leaving for a life of servitude? She was tempted to slash a T-shirt and don her oldest pair of jeans in order to effect that holey, threadbare look, but she restrained herself.

What was the point? She'd learned enough about Kane today to know that he wouldn't care what sort of costume she chose to depart in. He would only laugh and make some maddeningly droll or suggestive remark. But her parents would be aghast, the guests titillated, and as for herself—her proper, always perfectly attired self—she would end up embarrassed.

Carling heaved a disgusted sigh. She would choose something appropriate to wear. Since she was leaving civilization, she might as well go out in style. Stripping to her dusky rose teddy and sheer stockings, which were kept in place with lacy garters, she stood in front of her open closet, surveying the contents of her wardrobe.

The door to her room opened—she hadn't given a thought to locking it—and Kane walked in. They stared at each other, silent and still, for a long moment.

Five

___

Kane's burning gray eyes slid over her, taking in her mane of champagne-blond hair, which tumbled over her shoulders, her full breasts with their pointed crests, her small waist and the womanly curves of her hips. The lace and silk confection she wore was as feminine and delicate as her small-boned frame and accentuated all her charms.

He dropped his gaze to her long, shapely legs. The stockings ended provocatively at the tops of her thighs, which were firm and rounded. He imagined the softness between them and desire stabbed at him. His loins grew taut and heavy in response to the alluring sight of his bride. She combined a compelling sexuality with a graceful elegance, and the results were challenging and irresistible. Never could he remember wanting a woman this much.

He found the incredible hunger raging through him more than a little unnerving. For the first time that day, the usually unflappable Kane McClellan felt himself in danger of losing his head. Immediately, he forced himself to tear his gaze away from her, to rein the wildness coursing through his body.

It had been a long, long time since anyone or anything had had such a powerful effect upon him and the realization unsettled him. He was not the kind of man who lost control; he managed his passion, his temper, his ambition, his intelligence with razor-sharp precision. He hid his feelings behind a cool, often glib facade; open displays of emotion were not for him. Those men who wept to demonstrate their sensitivity gave him the creeps.

Kane McClellan did not indulge in self-disclosure. A born introvert, he'd combined his deeply ingrained reserve with a quiet assertiveness to which others invariably yielded. It seemed natural for him to be in charge and so, naturally, he always was, in both business and family matters.

He'd planned his marriage with the same unerring dedication to detail that had earned him a fortune, choosing a wife who filled his requirements: intelligent but not involved in a career, of good moral character, from a stable family background, attractive, a woman who shared his traditional values that a wife and mother's place was in the home. Living on a huge working ranch, far from any urban area, it couldn't be any other way. Carling Templeton fit the bill perfectly, right down to her public declarations about wanting lots of babies and staying home to care for them.

But he hadn't let himself fully consider the physical impact she'd had on him, choosing to relegate that to the background as he engineered the marriage. Never had it occurred to him that the mere sight of her would leave him aching and breathless. That wasn't in his plans! Kane McClellan was invulnerable, in business, family and love!

He'd always possessed the ability to swiftly and thoroughly assess a situation, and that talent didn't fail him now. He had no illusions about his bride's feelings. Should she discover that she was capable of arousing these wild feelings in him, that she had the mystifying power to send him spinning out of control...

Kane clenched his jaw and swallowed hard. The results would be disastrous—to him. No sane man would allow a woman to know he was vulnerable to her, particularly not a woman who claimed to hate him, who would use that knowledge as power to hurt him in every way she could. He wasn't about to put that kind of a weapon in her hands!

He was aware that Carling saw him as her captor, as an iron man in absolute control of her and in absolute control of himself. He had no intention of disabusing her of that image.

"Get out of my room," Carling snapped. She was still shaking from his frank and intensely sexual appraisal of her. She'd seen the penetrating hunger in his eyes and had read the desire there. He wanted her and he meant to have her. His arrogance, his confidence, his masculine size and strength, his determination—all of it terrified her.

But she didn't dare let him see her fear. It was better he think that he infuriated her than for him to know just how scared she really was. She wasn't about to put that kind of a weapon in his hands! At least her anger and disdain for him gave her some illusion of power and she needed that power, however illusory, to hold her own against Kane McClellan tonight.

"I came up to ask if you needed any help with your suitcases," he said, pleased with the calmness of his voice. He was back in control again, the momentary madness safely at bay. "Perhaps you need some help getting dressed instead?"

"No, thank you." Carefully avoiding looking at him, Carling snatched an ultrasuede skirt in a soft pumpkin shade from a hanger. It was short and straight and very fashionable.

She pulled on the skirt and stepped into her pumpkincolored suede shoes. The heels were very narrow and very high. Kane stood watching her, his gray eyes dark and burning.

The intensity of his gaze made her feel a little wild and that alarmed her. "Go back downstairs to our guests." She barked the order like a Marine drill instructor addressing the rawest recruit. "I'll be along when I'm ready."

"I'm sick of our guests. I'll stay here until you're ready to leave. And that's going to be momentarily." It was an order, not a statement.

Carling pulled on an ivory raw-silk blouse, her fingers fumbling with the delicate buttons. When Kane offered his assistance, she swatted his hands away. Undaunted, he slid one long finger under the thin strap of the teddy and lightly stroked her smooth white skin.

"So the Ice Princess has a predilection for sexy lingerie?" he murmured lightly. "What a pleasant surprise."

Carling shivered at his touch before she determinedly moved herself out of reach. "I chose my lingerie to please myself, not you!" she said fiercely.

"Isn't it fortunate that our tastes coincide?" His voice was low and deep. He watched her finish buttoning her blouse and put on a vest, which matched her skirt. A sudden smile crossed his face. "*Her Secret* specializes in lingerie, doesn't it? Sexy, feminine, expensive lingerie."

Carling pressed her lips together into a tight, straight line. It was humiliating to have to acknowledge the fact that he had paid for her lingerie, as if she were already his kept mistress.

"It affirms my belief in your passionate nature, Carly. If you were the dried-up prune you pretend to be, you would be wearing starched, opaque cotton underwear that contains and covers everything."

The intent in his eyes sent an unwilling, unwelcome heat rippling through her. Having him watch her dress made her feel positively lascivious. Worse, some primal, demented part of her actually wanted to preen under his hot gaze, to make her movements slow and sinuous...

Carling firmly suppressed the crazy and traitorous instinct.

She stormed over to her vanity table and grabbed her hairbrush, pulling it through her long, blond hair with quick, violent strokes. Her body language unmistakably reflected homicidal, not seductive intentions.

Kane watched her for a few moments, then turned to gaze around the room. It was a dainty, flowery feminine room, decorated in shades of pink and cream and mauve, with ruffled curtains and a canopied bed. He felt like an alien in it, as any male would.

And then his eyes focused on the corner cabinet, which was filled with... "Rabbits?" he exclaimed, walking over to investigate. All five shelves of the antique mahogany cabinet held small colorful rabbits, ceramic and porcelain and wooden ones in various poses and modes of dress.

"Good grief, a rabbit hutch!" He burst out laughing. "I've never seen so many rabbits in one place in my entire life!"

"A rabbit hutch?" Carling echoed. She decided that it would be useless to inform him of the cabinet's eighteenth century European origins. The barbarian could never appreciate the fact.

"I'm glad my collection amuses you," she said coldly. "I've been collecting since I've been six years old. Many of the figurines are antiques."

Kane was obviously not impressed. He was still laughing. "This is incredible. Pilgrim rabbits, Indian rabbits, rabbits wearing Hawaiian shirts and leis and holding ukeleles. And here's an entire school of bunnies, sitting at little desks with a teacher bunny standing by a little blackboard." He laughed harder.

"That wooden bunny school happens to be imported from West Germany. I fail to find anything funny about it or about my collection in general."

"The sight of a rabbit dressed like a Russian cossack or a Japanese geisha doesn't even bring a smile to your lips? A rabbit wearing a kilt and tam and holding a set of bagpipes doesn't strike you as hilarious?"

She raised her chin haughtily. "I have the complete set of twenty-four internationally costumed English bone china rabbits. It's twenty years old and priceless."

"Oh, it's priceless, all right!" His inflection gave the word an entirely different meaning. "Are you going to have the rabbit hutch and its inhabitants shipped to the ranch? Or keep them here—I hope."

"Oh, I'll definitely have them shipped to the ranch. In fact, I'll be sure to have the cabinet installed in your room. You'll hate that, won't you, Kane? All those cute little bunnies in your very own masculine domain."

"I've never been threatened with cute little bunnies before. You're really scaring me, honey." He chuckled, completely undaunted, making her feel even more foolish.

Her emotions roiling, she impulsively tossed her hairbrush at him. He caught it with one hand.

Kane stared at the brush, then at her, his dark eyebrows arched, his eyes narrowed to heavy-lidded slits. "Are you inviting me to use this on that saucy little bottom of yours?"

"Just try it." Carling's cheeks flamed a deep crimson. "Try it and I'll yell so loudly that everyone in this house will be up here to—"

"Watch me tame the shrew?"

"Oh, how I hate you!" she said breathlessly.

"So you keep saying. And I'm getting tired of hearing it." Still holding the brush, he advanced toward her, crossing the room in a few, long strides.

Carling tensed all over and began a retreat. She didn't know what he intended to do but whatever it was, she had to face the unpleasant fact that she'd driven him to it.

"No, Kane. Please don't!" She held up her hands to ward him off, but he merely used them to pull her close to him.

He stared down into her wide, apprehensive blue eyes. "Hmm, it seems that the shrew suddenly has been transformed into a scared little bunny rabbit. I guess this calls for a change in tactics." He dropped the brush and scooped her up in his arms. Holding her high against his chest, he headed for the door.

It was unsettling to be carried, to be high above the ground with no control over her own movements. Carling clutched at him in sheer self-preservation. "Kane, put me down. Where are we going? Let me go! I want to walk."

She kept up a running commentary as he strode from the room, through the hall and down the stairs, lapsing into mortified silence when he plowed through the cheering crowd, which had gathered to watch their departure.

"Her bags are upstairs in her room, if anybody wants to carry them out to the car," Kane announced with a charming smile.

His unexpected, previously unseen smile made an instant impact upon the guests. A group of both men and women trooped upstairs to do Kane's bidding.

With Carling still firmly ensconced in his arms, Kane swung open the front door. "Goodbye," he called cheerfully. "Y'all keep in touch now."

"Kane, we can't just leave!" cried Carling. "We didn't even say goodbye to Daddy and Mama yet."

"Sweetheart, I'm all for avoiding a big, tearful farewell scene. We'll call your folks tomorrow before we leave for the airport and say goodbye then."

But Clayton and Neva appeared in the front hall, having been notified by other guests of the couple's departure, and the tearful farewell scene that Kane had hoped to avoid began in earnest.

Neva and Carling embraced and wept openly. The senator hung behind, his blue eyes misting. Kane allowed for five full minutes of anguish and lamentations before he put his bride into the car, climbed behind the wheel and drove off with a jaunty honk of the horn.

"Alone at last," he said dryly, glancing over at Carling, who was sobbing into the lace handkerchief, which a thoughtful guest had pressed into her hand.

"How could you just drive away like that! My poor mother was—"

"Overreacting a bit. I did all of us a favor by leaving when she started into that 'what will Daddy and I do without our little girl?' stuff. You're twenty-eight, Carly, not fourteen. Most women your age have long since left the nest for their own homes and their own lives."

Carling's tears disappeared. Now she was too angry to cry. "I'm not interested in hearing your self-serving demographic statistics! Only an insensitive brute would fail to understand the distress Mama and I were feeling. And when I saw the stricken look on Daddy's face, I—"

"He looked relieved to me. When I told him to send me the bills for our wedding reception he looked downright ecstatic."

"Insensitive brute is too complimentary a term for a hard, cold, domineering tyrant like you." She was so infuriated with Kane that she forgot to be upset about leaving home.

Kane shrugged. "It's not the kind of compliment I especially enjoy receiving." He turned on the radio. "Shall we listen to my choice of music or do you have a station that you'd prefer?"

She wanted to ignore him, to brush him off with the cold-shoulder treatment. But if she didn't speak up, she'd be forced to listen to one of his country music tunes—and he'd have no compunction at all about *whistling* along. She decided to spare herself that.

She purposefully turned the dial to her favorite station, one that featured a format of "contemporary light rock, old and new." An old favorite from her college days was being played, and she settled back in the seat to listen.

Kane glanced at her. "You like that song?"

"Yes." She folded her arms across her chest and glared straight ahead. She had no intention of carrying the conversation any further, but midway through the song a kind of antagonistic curiosity forced her to ask, "Do *you* like it?'' And to add, just to be contrary: ''Because if you do, the song is ruined for me. I'll never listen to it again.''

''I never particularly cared for it but Missy, my girlfriend at the time when it was popular, loved it. She played the song so many times that whenever I hear it, I think of her.''

Carling considered what he had just said. And unexpectedly, her temper flared to flash point. ''You're sitting here with your *wife* on your *wedding day* thinking about another woman? Boasting about an old girlfriend? That's—that's reprehensible!'' She leaned forward and changed the dial to an all news station.

Kane's lips twitched with amusement. ''I wasn't boasting. Looking back, Missy was more nightmare than dream girl.''

''I'm certainly not interested in hearing about her.'' Carling tossed her head. ''I couldn't care less about anyone in your past, present or future.''

But privately, she admitted that her actions belied her words. Why, *why* did he affect her like this? Why should hearing about a song that reminded him of an old girlfriend make her blood boil? Carling resolutely refused to consider an answer to either question.

They arrived at the hotel/motel complex near the airport and Kane checked in. He noticed her five bulging suitcases for the first time, as the bellhop loaded them onto a gurney.

''I said to pack a suitcase or two, not everything you own,'' Kane grumbled as they followed the bellhop toward the elevator.

''It's not everything I own, not even half. I had to pack enough to last me until the Wells Fargo wagon straggles the whole way out to your ranch—and that could be months!''

''Carly, the ranch is in Texas, not Outer Mongolia. Our mail is delivered daily and not by Pony Express.'' He sounded exasperated.

Carling was delighted that she'd managed to pierce his air of unfaltering implacability. She wanted him to feel as off balance as he made her feel. It wasn't fair that she should become irrational and overemotional around him while he always maintained his cool!

But her bravado abruptly faded the moment they stepped into the living room of the enormous suite. Kane handed the bellhop a generous tip and the man smilingly departed, leaving the couple alone.

Carling's breath caught in her throat and she clenched her fingers into fists. This was it. Somehow she'd managed to get through the day without fully accepting the fact that she would end up in a bedroom with Kane McClellan tonight. Always in the back of her mind had been the possibility, the *certainty*, that she would somehow escape. But such denial was no longer possible.

She stood stock-still, her eyes round, her mouth dry, watching Kane explore the suite.

"This is called the presidential suite," he said, examining the complimentary fruit basket and bottle of champagne. "I chose it over the bridal suite because hotel decorators sometimes have a tendency to run amok when it comes to bridal suites. Round vibrating beds, fur throws, mirrors on the ceilings . . . I didn't think either of us would care for that."

Carling thought that if she were to walk into a bedroom and be faced with a round bed covered in fur and topped by a ceiling mirror, she would faint on the spot. As it was, she already felt dangerously light-headed.

She sank into a chintz-covered chair, and like a mouse eyeing a stalking cat, she vigilantly watched Kane's movements. Then her stomach growled. Carling closed her eyes and groaned inwardly. This was all she needed. In addition to feeling weak and weepy with anxiety, she was also starving. She hadn't eaten a thing all day.

Her eyes flew open the moment she sensed Kane's approach. He stood in front of her chair, looking down at her with intense gray eyes. "Are you all right?" he asked quietly.

Had he made a glib or snide remark, she might have mustered the strength to fight back. But his tone was devoid of any flippant sarcasm and his expression was neither taunting nor amused. It was serious and concerned.

Carling silently shook her head, afraid that if she were to risk speaking, she might inadvertently burst into tears instead.

Kane got down on his haunches in front of her and took both her hands in his. "Your hands are like ice." He uncurled her fingers and interlaced them with his own. He stood up and slowly, inexorably pulled her to her feet so that she was standing in front of him.

Carling gasped sharply as a wave of panic assailed her. "No, don't! I can't go through with it! I just can't!"

He lifted her right hand to his mouth and kissed each fingertip. "I was going to suggest ordering dinner," he said mildly. "I noticed that you managed to avoid the dried-up canapés and the rest of that overpriced slop at the party, just like I did."

"*Capitol Affairs* does not serve slop," Carling rallied herself to say. "Their veal ragout is legendary. But you have a point about the overpricing. They do, outrageously. Wait until you get their bill."

"Something to look forward to," he said wryly.

"You'll be shocked at the cost of the reception," she added with relish, permitting herself to enjoy that small revenge.

"I suppose I should gallantly remark that money is no object when it comes to my wedding day."

His tone was so droll that Carling almost smiled in spite of herself. Almost. She opted for a cool, blank stare instead.

Holding her hand, Kane led her over to the small desk where a menu had been placed conveniently near the telephone. "Tell me what you want from room service and I'll call down our order."

Carling ignored the menu; her eyes darted nervously around the suite once more. Dining here, alone with him, was entirely too intimate. "Why don't we go out for dinner?" she asked with what she hoped passed for spontaneous ingenuous charm. She even managed a bright smile. "You wanted to go to a restaurant and I know all the good ones in the area. Just tell me what kind of food you feel like eating and—"

"We're eating here," Kane said flatly. He picked up the telephone receiver. "I'm ordering a steak for myself. Shall I order the same for you or are you going to tell me what you want?"

"I want to get out of here! I want to go home!" she burst out.

"I meant what you wanted from the menu," Kane explained patiently.

His deliberate obtuseness maddened her. Seething with anger, she snatched the receiver from his hand and slammed it back into its cradle.

"Does that mean you'd rather postpone ordering dinner . . . until afterwards?" Kane asked silkily.

Too late Carling realized the consequences of her outburst. He'd given her the ideal opportunity to stall for time by suggesting room service and she'd thrown it away. "No, I—uh—" She cleared her throat. "I just needed a little more time to study the menu," she improvised hastily. She grabbed the menu and pretended to study it, all the while carefully inching away from him.

His big hand reached out to take the menu away from her. He let it fall to the floor. "Are you afraid of me or of sex in general?" he asked quietly.

"I'm not afraid!" Carling refuted at once. She couldn't admit to fear, not to him! One must appear brave in the face of the enemy. "I just don't particularly care for sex. It's nothing personal against you," she added quickly, not wanting either to anger or challenge him at this point. Common sense had replaced outrage, making her nervously aware of her own vulnerability—a woman alone in a hotel suite with a man much larger and stronger than she was. "I don't want it or like it with anybody."

"And what brought you to that conclusion?"

Her blue eyes searched his face for any signs of mockery, but his expression was totally enigmatic. She swallowed. "I tried it once. That was enough for me."

"Once?"

"One time ten years ago. I didn't care to repeat—" she paused as a flush of warm color suffused her cheeks "—it."

"You really are repressed," Kane marveled. "You can't even say the word." He shook his head. "Now, let me make sure I've got this straight—after one adolescent sexual experience, you decided to put your sexuality on ice? And that's what you've done for the past ten years?"

His undisguised incredulity made her feel like a freak. "I tried to warn you that I wasn't . . . good in bed but you refused to listen." She scowled at him, her tone defensive. And then an idea occurred to her. She might just have a chance to escape, after all. "But it's true. I'm an icicle. Being married to me would be like—like being permanently stuck in the Arctic Circle. You're perfectly justified to seek an annulment and I'll gladly cooperate in any way I can to facilitate—"

"Baby, give it up." Kane sighed. "There isn't going to be an annulment. And your self-enforced chastity ends right now." He cupped her chin with one hand and swept his other arm around her to pull her close to him. "I'm here to set you free."

The swiftness of his actions caught her off guard and before she could utter a plea, protest or insult, his mouth had descended on hers. Startled, she arched her back and tried to wiggle out of his hold, but his grip was inexorable. His hard mouth had already closed over hers and was forcing her lips apart. She felt his warm breath filling her mouth and then his tongue thrusting into the moistness, probing, caressing, teasing her own tongue as her senses reeled.

Carling tried to pull away, but Kane ignored her futile attempts, deepening the kiss and tightening his hold on her. It was impossible to break free, she acknowledged dizzily, and it was becoming increasingly difficult to think her way out of her predicament.

Her eyes closed involuntarily and she couldn't seem to marshall the strength to open them again. Helplessly, she felt herself being drawn into a whirling vortex where sensation, not thought, reigned supreme. His seductive mastery was far beyond her level of experience. She grew languid and weak and for a moment she lay limply against him. It was easier to let him kiss her as intimately as he wished than to try to rally her defenses.

He slipped his hand inside her vest and cupped her breast in his big hand. The dual layers of her silk teddy and blouse offered no defense against the exciting warmth of his palm. His fingers caressed her, teasing the soft tip of her breast into a hard, throbbing little bead. Carling gasped at the hot surge of pleasure that flowed through her.

"You're so responsive," Kane said raspily, lifting his lips from her mouth to trail a path of fiery kisses along the slender curve of her throat. He pushed aside the collar of her blouse to seek the sensitive areas of her shoulder. "Too warm and passionate to live without loving. It's time for you to learn what you've been missing."

"I haven't missed a thing," Carling protested huskily as he swung her up in his arms.

"I'll get your opinion on that later, after you've been to bed with me," Kane said with a sexy male smile.

Six

He carried her into the bedroom, which was tastefully decorated in neutral grays and blues. The bed was a standard king-size, without mirrors, fur throws or anything else that might not fit with the room's conservative decor. He set her on her feet and began to unbutton his shirt with the natural ease of someone not at all uncomfortable about undressing in front of others.

Other *women*, Carling amended silently. The drugging cloud of passion, which had temporarily engulfed her, lifted and she found herself facing cold, hard reality. Kane McClellan was an experienced man, smooth and sure of himself, not at all the socially inept bumpkin he'd been portrayed as—and which she'd wanted him to be! She had needed the sense of superiority such an image of him provided for her.

But here in the bedroom, as she watched him take off his shirt, his boots, socks and wide leather belt, Carling grimly admitted that *she* was the inept one. She was inexperienced and scared. All her sophisticated polish, her skill in sparkling party conversation, her cool elegance were useless in an intimate situation like this. Was that part of the reason why she'd been avoiding just such an encounter all these years?

She sucked in her breath and gulped back a nervous whimper. She had to do something, but what? Her brain worked feverishly but with surprising acuity. Fighting him physically only increased his resolve, she thought. It excited him, too. She needed to try another tactic, one that discouraged instead of challenged.

Passive resistance? What if she were to lie as still as a corpse, cold and unresponsive? Surely any hot-blooded man, particularly one as passionate and demanding as Kane, would be completely turned off by such a—well—dead response.

A small mirthless smile curved her lips. A man with his confidence, which all too often bordered on arrogance, wouldn't tolerate a woman who didn't melt in his arms. He wouldn't be able to let her go fast enough! She'd have to make sure to have him promise to forward the incriminating financial documents before he hustled her out the door.

"You're grinning like a cat who's just noticed that the door to the canary's cage is open. Care to share the joke?"

Kane's voice jolted her out of her pleasant revenge-and-rescue fantasy. He was standing directly in front of her, close enough to touch, too close *not* to touch. He was shirtless and the fit of his jeans had been altered by the insistent bulge beneath the heavy metal buttons of his fly.

"There isn't any joke." Her voice faltered. Unless it was on her, she said to herself, her eyes widening.

She wanted to look away from him, to run away, but she stood transfixed by the sight of him, by his sheer male power. His skin was smooth and golden from hours in the sun, his chest and shoulders broad and muscular. Dark hair covered his chest and arrowed downward, disappearing into the low-slung waistband of his jeans.

Kane's gaze followed hers. "Such great big scared eyes," he murmured softly. "Just like a quivering little bunny rabbit."

"Don't make fun of me!" It was supposed to be an order, but her voice didn't contain the necessary defiance to make it sound like one. To Carling's horror, she realized she'd sounded as if she were pleading with him instead.

Kane apparently thought so, to. "No, sweetheart, I won't hurt you. You're my wife, I'll never be cruel to you."

He stepped closer and took her hand, pressing it against his straining masculinity and holding it there when she reflexively tried to draw back. "Feel how much I want you." His voice was low and deep and almost hypnotic in intensity. "That's what happens to me when I look at you, when I kiss you and touch you. I want you, Carly."

He brushed her lips with his, lightly, provocatively, tantalizing and sensitizing, but not consuming her mouth with the ardent hunger of his previous kisses. "I want you."

A powerful combination of curiosity, confusion and desire burned within her, so intermingled that she couldn't begin to separate one from the other. But there was one emotion that was fast receding in the onslaught of the other three. And that was fear.

He felt hard and heavy under her hand, so foreign, so male. Hesitant but unwittingly fascinated, she relaxed her fingers and permitted herself to feel the rigid shape of him beneath the cloth.

Kane made a sound from deep in his throat. "Not yet, baby," he gritted out hoarsely. "Not now. We're going to have to go slowly this time." He carefully but firmly removed her hand and placed it on his chest.

It took sheer willpower for him to put on the brakes, but being Kane, he did so without hesitation. Her admitted sexual inexperience and apprehension evoked all his strong protective instincts. Carling belonged to him now. She was his wife and she needed to be soothed and taken slowly, regardless of the ferocity of his own needs. Those long years she'd spent in sexual hibernation made her much younger in terms of experience than her chronological age.

"There's nothing to be afraid of," he gasped. "I'm going to take care of you. I'll give you all the words and the kisses and the petting you need. It's going to be good for you, I promise."

He bent his head and kissed her.

This time she opened her lips to him automatically. His tongue delved inside to stroke her mouth, slowly, luxuriously. His hands moved over her back and then around and under her vest. He slipped it off her shoulders and let it drop to the floor. Carling barely noticed. The ribbon of heat uncurling in her belly claimed her full attention. It grew deeper and hotter as his hands rubbed the sides of her breasts through the cool silk.

Her fingers curled into the soft mat of hair, learning its texture, exploring the sinewy muscles beneath. She vaguely remembered her plan of not responding to him, but somehow neither active nor passive resistance seemed as compelling as it had earlier. A growing hunger for the feel of his hands on her naked breasts was overwhelming all rational thought. The double silk barrier of her clothing was becoming intolerable; her nipples were tight and tingling and aching for his touch.

When his fingers finally moved to the buttons of her blouse, she uttered a breathless, incoherent cry of anticipation. Kane's fingers immediately stilled. "Not yet?" he whispered, his lips against hers. "I won't undress you until you're ready, darling. We're not going to rush."

His hands resumed their torment, taking care to keep her clothing chastely in place while his mouth claimed hers in another deep, intoxicating kiss.

Carling twisted restlessly against him, wrapping her arms around his neck and running her hands through the springy thickness of his hair. She was acting on pure instinct, trying to get closer to him, aching with a growing need and emptiness she had never before experienced.

Kane felt her frustration build and a smile curved his lips as his mouth left hers to nibble on her neck. He had deliberately misinterpreted that wild little cry of hers; he wanted her to be more than ready, he wanted her to be burning for him. And if she was feeling frustrated, it was only fair because he felt as if the top of his head was about to come off from all those potent kisses. In fact, his whole body throbbed from the evocative force of the teasing, arousing caresses.

He hadn't indulged in a good old-fashioned necking session since his teens and now he knew why. It was murder on the nerves and required incredible stamina; any sensible adult male would choose to consign all of that to his past and proceed directly to intercourse. But he wasn't feeling very sensible right now. One could rightly say that he'd never been sensible when it came to Carling Templeton, beginning with his compelling interest in her from her pictures to assuming her father's large debt, the first unprofitable financial move in his life.

But it was all going to work out all right, Kane assured himself uneasily. He could absorb the senator's debts without economic hardship and he could control these excessive, inconvenient *feelings* Carling unexpectedly evoked within him. He felt sure that once he had sated himself in her creamy softness, the raging fever in his blood would cool. He intended to have sexual satisfaction in his marriage, but he had no intention of becoming absurdly besotted with his wife.

Still, his control was becoming harder to maintain. It took considerable restraint to slowly undo the first three buttons of her blouse. His instincts were to rip it off her, but he remembered his pledge not to frighten her. He paused, to bolster his flagging control. And when he did, Carling's trembling fingers finished the job of unbuttoning her blouse for him.

Their eyes met for a long, charged moment.

"Take them off," Kane ordered softly. "The blouse and the skirt. Now."

The rational part of her brain immediately registered a protest. Wasn't it enough that he'd blackmailed her into marrying him and was now intent upon exercising his full marital rights, despite her own objections to both? Now he expected her to aid in her own seduction?

It was all so calculating, so domineering, she thought wildly, an angry despair growing within her. He'd take everything, her freedom, her body, her self-control, but that wasn't enough for him. He expected her to hand over her mind and her will to him, too.

And she was almost on the verge of doing just that. She'd actually unbuttoned her blouse right in front of him! A flush stained her cheekbones and Carling caught the edges of her open blouse and held them together, to protect her breasts from his penetrating gray eyes. A civil war was raging within her, willpower and pride on one side, desire and need on the other.

She shook her head. "No."

"I should button up your blouse and resume the kissing and the petting-outside-the-clothes routine until you're sobbing with frustration. Then you'll strip for me without a murmur of dissent." His voice was as hard and hungry as his eyes.

That would be the ultimate power play, he knew, but he also knew that he wasn't up to it. The effect she was having on him, *he* might end up being the one sobbing with frustration, long before she did!

"But this is neither the time nor the place for game playing. If you won't or can't take off your clothes, then I'll do it for you." He slipped the blouse from her shoulders, then unbuttoned and unzipped her skirt and pushed it over her hips. This time Carling stood before him in the dusky rose teddy, the sheer stockings and the high, high heels.

She was immobilized by a combination of horror, anxiety and embarrassment. Yet battling that volatile trio of emotions was a suppressed excitement, so fierce in its intensity that holding back became more difficult than giving into it.

The internal conflict left her reeling. What had he done to her? What was she doing to herself? "You'll be sorry for this," she said shakily, and immediately suppressed a groan. She, Carling Templeton, noted for her quick, sharp repartee had been reduced to spouting a cliché straight out of a low-budget movie.

"No, I won't." Kane's lips twisted into a small, reckless smile. His eyes were gleaming. "And neither will you. I intend to make sure of that."

Carling wasn't ready to let him. Realizing that she didn't have enough time to run around the bed, she attempted to scramble across it. Was she running away from him or enticing him to follow, to catch her? She was too overwhelmed to venture a guess.

The king-size bed seemed as huge as a football field and any hopes she'd entertained of reaching the other side came to an abrupt stop when his fingers closed firmly around her ankle. She went sprawling flat on her stomach, her arms and legs outstretched. Before she could catch her breath, he'd rolled her over onto her back and straddled her.

Gasping for air, Carling stared up at him with glittering blue eyes.

Their gazes met and held.

"Stop fighting me," Kane ordered softly.

"I won't." She arched beneath him. "I can't."

"Yes, you can. And you will." He reached down to cup the soft swells of her breasts with his big hands.

His caressing fingers were deft and strong and she felt her nipples grow so hard and so sensitive that she cried out. She couldn't lie still, she twisted beneath his hands willing him to stop but praying that he wouldn't. She wasn't aware that she'd flexed knees until she felt him lift her thigh and fit it snugly onto his hip. Instinctively, unthinkingly, she wrapped her other leg around him. The strength and tension vibrating from his hard masculine frame was as powerful an intoxicant as a gallon of moonshine.

His hands left her breasts to run along the smooth, long length of her legs. When he reached her feet, still encased in the pumpkin-colored suede heels, a rakish grin slashed his face. "Until I saw you in these, I never realized how sexy shoes could be. Do you want to leave them on?"

She shifted her leg, grazing him with the tip of the high, narrow heel. "They make an effective weapon," she murmured. She could certainly do some damage with them, so why didn't she? While she pondered her disturbing passivity, Kane slipped the shoes from her feet and tossed them to the floor.

"You don't need a weapon to use against me," he said, rolling down her silk stockings one at a time, then deftly divesting her of her garters.

Carling lay there, her breathing ragged, her heart pounding so wildly and so hard that the beats resounded in her head. His hands smoothed up and down her legs, and she felt the tight knot of desire growing, throbbing and burning in her abdomen and between her thighs.

She realized that somewhere along the line, she'd lost the inclination to escape and had begun to accept her fate. Was it because she was twenty-eight years old and tired of living a life of celibacy? Was it because she was a normal woman who had finally stopped repressing her normal urges?

It was a nice theory, but Carling was honest enough with herself to admit that it wasn't entirely true. Kane McClellan was the determining factor in her acquiescence. Though she'd tried to fight it, she had responded to him from the start; all her protestations were rendered irrelevant when she went wild in his arms. He was experienced and confident enough to separate her verbal hostility from her physical responses, abiding by the old axiom "Actions speak louder than words."

The thought galled her. Why, how, could a man she loathed make her feel this way, make her want... "It isn't right, it isn't fair," she blurted out.

"All's fair in love and war," Kane countered smoothly. He traced the circle of her navel through the cool silk of her teddy.

Just the touch of his fingertip sent shivers of desire rippling through her. Love. Merely hearing the word on his lips sent a bewildering surge of some unidentifiable emotion through her. It was anger, Carling decided resolutely. It had to be.

"This is war, all right," she snapped, struggling to sit up. It was impossible to do, given that his thighs were straddling her hips, but she kept trying. "Because the word *love* will never be used between you and me."

He put his hands on her shoulders and firmly pushed her down flat upon the mattress. "I'll keep that in mind," he said, lowering himself on top of her.

His lips took hers, teasing and coaxing until her mouth opened under his and when his tongue touched hers, she moaned. His body was covering hers; her softness absorbed the full, warm weight of him. She felt the seductive abrasiveness of his hair, the smooth, muscled hardness of his skin. Instinctively, her arms encircled him and she drew him even closer.

They kissed. Slow, ardent, hungry kisses, which grew longer and deeper and more intimate. After a long while, his lips left hers to draw the tip of one of her tightly budded breasts deeply into his mouth. He sucked it hard and the sound of Carling's moans of pleasure, of arousal filled the room. She felt lost in a world of pure sensation, the likes of which she had never even imagined.

And then he moved away from her, sitting up on the bed and leaving her lying alone and bereft across the mattress. Without thinking or caring what she was giving away or giving into, Carling gave a desperate little cry and reached out her arms to him. "Don't leave me," she begged in a throaty, sexy voice, speaking words she had never spoken before in a tone she had never heard herself use.

Kane smiled at the sound of it. "I won't," he promised. "I'm not."

Her eyes opened a slit and she watched him shuck off his jeans and briefs. Completely nude, he moved toward her again. Carling's eyes opened wider. Her only other sexual experience had been in the dark, with clothing hastily rearranged, not removed. This was her first sight of a fully aroused, mature naked male.

Her mouth went dry and when he came down beside her, she stiffened. He was so big, so strong, so nerve-shatteringly masculine. A wave of panic swept over her. What was she doing here? And how was she going to get away?

Kane propped himself up on one elbow and gazed intently at her. "Scared?" He stroked her cheek lightly.

Carling gulped. "I—I guess it's too late to holler 'rape.'"

He smiled. "I guess it is." His big hand slid caressingly over the curves of her body and came to rest at the juncture of her thighs. Still holding her eyes with his, he moved his hand between her legs.

"Then how about 'help'?" she asked breathlessly, trying to cross one leg over another in an attempt to avoid his long, probing fingers.

Her efforts were futile. He moved his thigh between hers, effectively opening her to him. Carling blushed as he reached for the hidden snaps of her silk teddy, which was moist with evidence of her desire.

"Why don't you try saying 'I want you,'" Kane suggested as he swiftly, deftly undid the snaps. He eased off the garment, his eyes studying her nakedness. "You're beautiful, Carly," he murmured. "So soft and feminine. So— *beautiful*," he repeated, his voice husky.

The word somehow seemed inadequate, but his mind was spinning too fast to run through a list of synonyms. She was all softly rounded curves and hollows, her skin smooth and white, the tips of her breasts pink, the dark, downy thatch hiding the secret folds of her femininity. And she was his. His woman; his wife. He felt proud and possessive.

A fierce, unexpected tenderness welled up within him, surprising him. It was all so foreign to him. He knew himself to be responsible and dependable, he would admit to being dominating and aggressive at times, and passionate, too, when the circumstances were right. But tender? He was amazed by the feelings sweeping through him, by the words he suddenly wanted to say to her, by the things he wanted her to say to him.

Somehow it was no longer enough that he had her in his bed, physically ready to admit him inside her. He wanted more. He wanted to hear her say the words. He needed those words, he realized, his astonishment growing.

Carling felt hot all over. The intensity of his gaze felt as heated as a flame. That he should have such intimate knowledge of her was as daunting as it was thrilling. She didn't understand how it was possible to feel so weak and languorous, yet so vibrant and alive, all at the same time.

"Say it, Carly. Tell me that you want me." It was a command, and Carling instantly rebelled. He was poised over her, watching her with hooded eyes.

"No." Who was she fighting, him or herself? a nagging little voice in her head taunted. She had no secrets from Kane McClellan, not now. He had seen her, touched her... he knew. Oh, he knew exactly how aroused she was and how much she wanted him. But, dammit, she wasn't about to tell him so. He couldn't have it all his way. "No," she repeated stubbornly.

Unexpectedly, Kane laughed. "You're a feisty one, bunny rabbit. Your body has already surrendered and we both know it. You're hot and wet and ready for me. Why won't you admit it?" His voice grew coaxing and seductive. "Say that you want me."

It was the voice of the serpent suggesting that Eve take just one tiny bite of the shiny red apple, Carling thought grimly. She closed her eyes. "I won't ever say that."

"You will," he said with his usual confidence.

Or was it determination? Carling wasn't sure; with Kane they sometimes seemed one and the same.

And then he touched the feathery softness between her thighs. Her body arched spasmodically against his hand and he smiled with pure male satisfaction. She wanted him, and badly, even if she wouldn't admit it. Yet.

He continued to caress the soft, swollen warmth of her, exploring the secret folds, delving deeper, rubbing, pressing, stroking rhythmically. Heat waves of pleasure spiraled from deep within the feminine center. Carling clutched his shoulders, her nails biting into his muscled flesh. She moaned and tossed her head back and forth, consumed by a fierce, delicious urgency she had never experienced before. Her eyes were closed, her lips parted, her breath came in short, sharp gasps.

Her mind seemed to be splintering away as she surrendered to the unbearably wonderful sensations pulsating through her. Her whole body began to quiver and a fine sheen of perspiration covered her skin.

"You want me. Say it, Carly."

Kane's voice swirled in the velvet mist surrounding her. Once again, it was a demand, but this time a demand from him did not incite her to rebel. Instead, she wanted to give to him, she wanted to please him. It was all so new to her, the flowing passion, the dependence, the soft need to yield. She gave into it, into him.

"Yes," she whispered, clinging to him. "Yes, I want you."

She was out of control and it was exciting, exhilarating, as if she were breaking out of prison. Her body tensed and then went rigid as a hot shower of sparks exploded within her. Her moans turned into cries of ecstasy and she convulsed helplessly around his fingers.

Tears of release stained her face and Carling lay nearly insensate with bliss, wanting nothing more than to lie alone in silence and savor the languid glow radiating through her.

Kane's voice, coming from somewhere above her, was an unwelcome intrusion into her pleasurable state of erotic solitude.

"Open your eyes, Carly."

She did so, reluctantly. He was poised over her, his mouth twisted into a wry smile. "Your nap will have to wait, sweetheart. You're not through for the night yet."

She felt the hard thrust of his manhood against her. She couldn't look at it or at him. "I'm afraid," she murmured. But she lay still, her legs apart and open, making no move to get away from him.

"I know, baby." He acknowledged her anxiety, but didn't offer to end it by letting her go. Nor did she suggest it. It was time; his possession was inevitable. An odd relief surged through her as she acknowledged it.

He entered her easily. She arched upward, expecting pain but there was none. She could feel him filling her with his masculine power and strength. She could feel her body reflexively accommodating him. And still there was no pain.

He moved within her, slowly at first as she adjusted and accepted all of him, then deeper and faster and harder as her body instinctively matched his rhythm. In and out, over and over again. Each time he withdrew from her she ached with an emptiness that only his hard male heat could alleviate. She felt the exquisite tension build inside her again, felt the incredible pleasure flare through her once more.

She wrapped herself around him and clung to him, crying his name. She didn't know what was happening to her or how or why, she only knew that she wanted him inside her, again and again, deeper and harder, more of him, all of him.

The wild, savage passion surged through her, expanding in hot rhythmic waves, sweeping both of them into the tumultuous seas of rapture. When the final shimmering tremors of release ebbed, Kane collapsed on top of her in a state of unadulterated satisfaction. Carling held him tight.

She felt weak and utterly replete, too dreamy and dazed to do anything but lie beneath him, clinging to him.

When Kane finally pulled away from her to lie on his back beside her, she had to force herself to swallow a cry of protest. She was shocked to realize how much she still wanted him on her, and in her.

The golden afterglow began to fade and the first unsettling twinges of reality set in. Carling made herself open her eyes. The sight of her naked body lying across the big bed, flushed and damp from the passionate consummation of their marriage, struck her as shockingly wanton. Vivid, sensual memories filled her brain, so real that she could actually taste his kisses, feel his hands on her, feel him moving inside her.

Carling sat up, her face crimson. Kane rolled over onto his side, watching her intently. She had to drag her eyes away from his long, hard body. *That* part of him looks so very different now . . . after. She drew in a ragged breath.

He traced the straight, sensitive line of her spine with the tip of one long finger, and sensual shivers rippled through her.

"Lie down with me." His voice was huskily inviting.

"I just did. Now I—I want to take a shower." Her mind was mired in a bog of confusion. She needed to be alone to clear it. But when she tried to move out of his reach, his hand snaked out to seize her wrist.

"I'll overlook your lack of bedroom etiquette since all of this is so new to you." With one easy movement, Kane pulled her down and over his body, then held her there with arms of steel. "But you can definitely use a couple of basic lessons. Bedroom Etiquette Lesson One—don't go racing off to the shower immediately after making love. Your partner is liable to think that you can't wait to wash away all traces of him."

He shifted her slightly, to better absorb the cushiony softness of her weight. "Makes a bad impression, you know?" He grinned at her, inviting her to share the humor.

She wasn't in the mood to be playful. Carling tried to twist free, but his grip remained firm. Lying on top of him like this gave her an entirely different view of his virility and she was finding it increasingly difficult not to savor it and revel in it.

What was the matter with her? she wondered bleakly. How could she still respond to him, still want him when her body hadn't yet recovered from his first powerful possession of her? Worse, he was her avowed enemy, the man she hated most in the world!

"Let me go," she said desperately. Then she swallowed hard and forced herself to add, "Please. I just need a little time and space. To be alone for a while."

He appeared to consider it. "You want time and space to start rebuilding those walls that came tumbling down tonight. To convince yourself that I'm a treacherous, manipulative villain who made you do all kinds of things you didn't want to do."

"You did! You are!" she exclaimed. And then, to remind herself as well as him, she added wildly, "I hate you!"

She tried to fight him for her freedom, but he easily subdued her by simply rolling over and pinning her beneath him. He was so strong, so big. Her breathing began to grow rapid and shallow. He was so virile and hard. Not to mention treacherous and manipulative.

She squirmed as her body began to tighten and throb in response to his nearness. The wiry-soft mat of hair on his chest tickled her breasts, her thighs were entangled with his. She moved again, but he didn't loosen his hold. Her insides were melting. How could she be expected to fight him and win? He was bigger and stronger and far more experienced than she was. Of course he could make her do all kinds of things she didn't want to do. He was making her feel like doing them right now! It was so easy to blame him for her acquiescence instead of herself and she gladly did so.

Kane glanced down at her. Her eyes were heavy-lidded and starting to close. Her body had begun to move sinuously against his. She might be too stubborn to admit it or even to realize it, but she wanted him as much as he wanted her. But her words rang unpleasantly in his ear. I hate you! Not exactly what a man wanted to hear from his bride on his wedding night, particularly not after what they'd just shared.

Frowning, he suddenly levered himself up. "I'm going to order that steak dinner now," he announced, padding naked into the sitting room of the suite. "I'll order the same for you," he called out.

Carling lay alone, too startled by his sudden departure to say a word. With effort, she raised herself on her elbows and stared vacantly into space. She knew it was absurd, but she felt like bursting into tears.

Kane appeared in the doorway a few moments later. She was sitting on the edge of the bed, wondering what to do next, trying to keep her tears and her thoughts at bay. She saw him survey her with cool gray eyes.

"Now might be a good time for Bedroom Etiquette Lesson Two," he said with enviable smoothness and calm. "Saying 'I hate you' in bed tends to alienate rather than entice a lover. A useful fact to keep in mind." He walked into the bathroom and closed the door behind him.

A moment later, she heard the sound of running water. "I said *I* wanted to take a shower first," she muttered aloud. It occurred to her that if they were a normal couple sharing a normal wedding night, she might slip into the shower and join him there. She'd seen enough movies to be able to picture the scene—the two of them standing under the spray of the water, making a rich lather from the soap and running caressing hands over each other's bodies. But in light of her newly acquired experience, she carried the fantasy a step further... Closing her eyes, she pictured him reaching for her, lifting her, entering her....

Carling's eyes flew open. She didn't know how, she admitted, her body vibrating with frustration. Was it actually physically possible to make love standing up? The more she tried to envision it, the more frustrated she became. Furious with herself for even considering it in the first place, Carling grabbed her indigo silk kimono from her suitcase and jerked it on, tying the sash firmly around her.

If she kept this up, she would be ready for a room with rubber walls, she thought crossly. And she'd be bouncing off every one of them. Kane chose that moment to emerge from the bathroom, a white towel tied around his waist.

Carling's heart jumped into her throat. If he came near her—if he tried to touch her—

He didn't. "The bathroom's all yours," he said with sickening cheerfulness. "Better make it snappy, though. Dinner should be here any minute." Whistling, he dropped the towel and strolled over to his canvas overnight bag.

Carling watched him, her eyes focused on his nude, muscular frame. She took a small step toward him and cleared her throat. Kane appeared to be oblivious of her presence as he rummaged through his bag.

It was as if he were alone in the room. He pulled on a pair of briefs, walked to the window and adjusted the curtains, then went back to search through his bag. He never glanced once in her direction. Tilting her chin at an imperious angle, Carling stalked grandly into the bathroom. She slammed the door so hard that the mirror shook, and she made sure to turn the lock with a loud click.

From the other side of the door, she heard that damn tuneless whistling of his. Kane hadn't reacted at all to her burst of temper. He hadn't come after her, hadn't even *looked* at her! Well, what had she expected? A terrible chilling wave of despair washed over her. Since he'd already had her, he felt no need to pursue her. He wasn't interested in what she was feeling or why.

Carling stepped into the shower and turned on the taps full blast. The water sluicing over her face, over her body effectively masked the tears streaming down her face. She didn't know why she was crying or why she felt so miserable. It certainly wasn't because she wanted Kane McClellan to come after her, to hold her in his arms and comfort her, to soothe away her tears and anger and confusion. Never that!

If he dared to break down the bathroom door and snatch her from the shower, she would hit him and kick him and bite him . . . Her stomach lurched. She'd bitten his shoulder tonight while caught up in the full throes of passion. She could remember the wildness coursing through her as his bold fingers worked their magic. She could remember writhing and moaning and finally sinking her teeth into his hard flesh because the urgency and fire were driving her out of her head. It was scary to think she'd been so out of control.

Carling felt hot and flushed, despite the cool temperature of the water. What was even scarier was that she wanted to feel that way again.

Seven

"**W**e'll be landing in a few minutes." Kane leaned over to give Carling's shoulder a gentle shake.

She jerked awake and stared around the cockpit of the small plane with dazed, drowsy eyes. It had seemed as if only moments ago they'd boarded the Cessna 310 with Kane at the controls. All the way to the airport she had protested the arrangements, reiterating her fear and dislike of private planes, casting aspersions on his abilities as a pilot.

At first Kane had attempted to reassure her, citing a study of safety statistics involving small planes and telling her the number of hours he'd flown during the fifteen years he'd had his pilot's license. When she had continued her litany of complaints, he had pointedly ignored her, bundling her and her luggage into the plane in his customary high-handed way.

During takeoff and their first fifteen minutes in the air, Carling waited with a kind of fatalistic dread for the plane to plummet in flames to the earth. When it didn't crash, she went on to anticipate a horrible bout of airsickness. But she didn't get sick, not even mildly queasy. Kane handled the controls with competency and ease. The plane flew smoothly, and her thoughts had turned to other things.

Like last night. Her cheeks turned pink and she glanced covertly at Kane, who was reading the instrument panel, unaware of her scrutiny.

Last night, her wedding night....

She had emerged from the shower, appalled that she'd cried and determined to never succumb to tears and weakness again. Kane might have won a victory of sorts by taking her to bed, but she hadn't lost the war yet. Nor would she! Before she could formulate any sort of plan, before she even had a chance to decide what clothes to put on, Kane had called from the other room that their dinners had arrived.

Carling flushed at the memory. She'd been starving, so hungry that she'd reacted without thinking, simply dropping her bath towel and slipping into her indigo silk kimono to rush to the table. Looking back, it was embarrassing that she'd been governed by such a common, elemental urge as hunger. It seemed so primitive, so physical, and she was *not* a person controlled by physical urges, she assured herself.

Still, to her discomfiture, she had to admit that she hadn't given a thought as to how Kane might interpret her appearing at the dinner table in nothing but a short, skimpy robe. At the time, her thoughts had been fixed solely on the steak dinner and her hunger pangs, which were so strong that they actually caused her pain.

If she closed her eyes now, she could visualize the small table set up in the suite with the snowy white tablecloth, the candlelight, the bottle of wine chilling in a sterling silver ice bucket. Carling nearly groaned aloud at the memory. It was a setting for seduction and she'd been the proverbial sitting duck. The food had been delicious, her wineglass had been liberally refilled throughout the meal and Kane had been attentive. So very attentive . . .

She'd felt so mellow after they'd finished the meal that she hadn't even offered a token protest when Kane had scooped her up in his arms. If he had taken her into the bedroom, she might have marshaled a defense, but instead he'd sat down on the long, cushioned sofa with her on his lap, talking to her, stroking her hair.

He'd caught her completely off guard. After all, one would expect a conservative, traditional man like Kane McClellan to confine his lovemaking to a bed in a bedroom. Not on a *sofa!* And by the time he'd begun kissing her, by the time he'd slipped his hands inside her kimono to touch her quivering, aching flesh, it had been too late. Her willpower had melted in the heat of his caresses, her resolution to resist him obliterated by the force of her desire.

Behind her burning eyelids, she could see herself shrugging the open kimono off her shoulders. In a kind of mental instant replay, she watched herself, naked and languorous, lying down on the sofa. She could almost feel the thick, chintz-covered cushions against her bare back and the solid weight of Kane's hard body upon her . . .

"We're down." The sound of Kane's voice startled her so much that she jumped. She'd been completely lost in those potent, erotic memories.

Blushing, she looked out and saw that they were on the ground and taxiing along a paved runway—in the middle of nowhere. Resentment flared anew. "I can't believe we're really here," she said. "I don't want to believe it."

"In a snit because all your dire predictions about flying in a small plane with me as the pilot didn't come true?" He took her hand and lifted it to his mouth, pressing his lips against her palm. "The flight was so smooth and I'm such a capable pilot that you relaxed completely. You slept for most of the trip."

She jerked her hand away. "I still have no faith in your rattletrap plane and even less in your so-called piloting abilities. And I didn't fall asleep because I was relaxed. I slept because I was totally exhausted. You kept me awake half the night!''

Kane laughed. Carling covered her mouth with her hands, aghast at her outburst. Why on earth had she brought up last night? The last thing she wanted was to rehash *that* with *him!*

"I was in top form last night, wasn't I?" He grinned wickedly. "Four times, hmm? Five, if you count this morning."

"You were relentless, and I don't mean that as a compliment!"

"Well, I'm taking it as one because you were with me all the way, baby. And that's what's driving you crazy, isn't it? All your convictions-set-in-concrete crumbled last night. You're neither the frigid ice princess nor the prim, fastidious maiden lady you thought you were. You're earthy and sexy and passionate and you loved everything we did together. In bed and out."

She sat stiffly in her seat, his words hitting her like stinging slaps. "Stop this plane. I want to get out!"

It was an effective exit line, only because the plane was already grinding to a halt. Scowling fiercely, she fumbled with the metal latch keeping the door shut.

"Wait a minute." Kane pulled her back to face him, and her traitorous nervous system went into overdrive at his nearness. The last time she'd been this close to him, she had been nude and so had he.

She blocked the thought and started to struggle. "Let me go!"

"Not until I tell you that my little sister is meeting us here to drive us back to the house. I radioed her shortly before landing. For Holly's sake, I'd like you to try to look more like a conventional bride and less like a combative prisoner."

"I am a prisoner! Stop trying to trivialize what you've done to me!"

"Maybe you could enlighten me," he said mildly. "Exactly what have I done to you?"

He was smiling, the snake. Carling wanted to scream with rage. "You bought me, as if I were a commodity on the open market. Do you know how it feels to know that you—you own me?"

"Judging from your responses last night—and this morning—I'd have to guess that it feels wonderful."

He'd struck a nerve, so Carling struck him. But he was expecting it and moved so lithely that she managed only a slight cuff to his shoulder. "You've ruined my life!" she cried, panting with fury. "And now I'm going to do my best to ruin yours!"

"Thanks for the warning. I'll be sure to be on guard. And as much as I'd like to continue our discussion, we're going to have to postpone it for now. There's Holly." Kane reached across her, unlatched the door and pushed it open.

"Kane!" cried a slender brunette with short dark hair and big gray-blue eyes. She was standing near a green station wagon. She jumped up and down and waved her arms when the plane's door swung open.

Carling stared at her. Kane's twenty-two-year-old sister Holly was about five feet eight inches tall, definitely too tall to be described as pixieish, but she had a certain elfin quality all the same. She was wearing jeans, boots and a blue and white checked Western-style shirt, proper ranch attire to be sure.

Carling smoothed the pleats of her short, red knit skirt, which, along with her red, white and blue cotton sweater and red high heels were as far from proper ranch attire as one could get. She looked ready to hit the mall, not ride the range.

Holly ran to the plane and stuck her head inside. She was beaming. "You have to be Kane's wife, Carly!" she exclaimed joyfully. "Oh, I'm so thrilled to meet you. And so surprised. I didn't know Kane even knew you. And he never mentioned that he was getting married. He never even mentioned that he was seriously dating anyone! I just screamed when he radioed me that he was arriving with his wife. Wait until Scott and Tim find out!''

Carling felt her mouth arrange itself into a smile. "Hello, Holly. It's nice to meet you, too,'' she heard herself say with the credible sincerity of a seasoned political campaigner.

Why? some submerged, rebellious part of her howled. Why did she always, always act as if she were seeking votes for her father? Why did she smile when she felt like spitting with rage? Why did she invariably utter polite, conventional phrases when she was thinking something else entirely? Only with Kane had she ever been able to express what she was really thinking and feeling. Terrific, she thought glumly. I can only be myself with my worst enemy.

"Let's get her bags into the car, Holly,'' Kane said, as he began to unload the luggage from the plane. Holly good-naturedly grabbed them and began to stuff them into the back of the station wagon.

Carling watched. She supposed that she should help, but loading and unloading bags was not her particular forte. As a senator's daughter, she'd always had someone around to handle such tasks. There had always been someone around to help her in and out of vehicles, too, but when Kane came to lift her from the plane, she quickly brushed him off and hopped down, unassisted.

Holly took the wheel of the car and Kane sat in the back seat, so close to Carling that his shoulder touched hers and his leg pressed against her thigh. His arm was firmly around her, and every time she tried to inch away from him, he moved right with her, as if he were glued to her. Her wriggling caused her skirt to creep slowly up her thighs.

When she saw Kane staring at her legs with *that* familiar gleam in his eye, she tugged the skirt down, feeling flustered and vulnerable. He had watched her dress this morning, had seen her don her red lace bra and panties, the red garter belt and sheer stockings. Carling shifted uneasily in the seat, feeling hot with shame. She hadn't tried to cover herself then; it was as if she'd *wanted* him to watch her.

She straightened abruptly and pulled her skirt down farther, primly arranging it over her knees. She hadn't wanted to entice him, she insisted stubbornly to herself. She'd simply been too tired to indulge in the fight she knew would ensue if she'd tried to send him out of the room while she was dressing.

"Tell me everything!" Holly cried, as she drove them away from the airstrip and small hangar. "When you met, how you met. When you decided to get married. Oh, Kane, this is the most exciting, romantic thing you've ever done." She paused and added incredulously. "Actually, it's the only exciting and romantic thing you've ever done."

"I'll let my beautiful bride fill you in on all the romantic details, Holly," Kane said, leaning down to brush Carling's temple with his lips.

"If I had any talent for creating romantic fiction, I'd be writing romance novels," Carling muttered in a low voice meant for Kane's ears only. "Although this marriage falls more into the realm of the horror genre. *You* tell her our bloodcurdling story."

Kane merely smiled and launched into a bare-bones recital of their first meeting at a political rally for Senator Templeton and their alleged long-distance secret romance, which had culminated in their elopement yesterday.

"It's wonderful," said Holly, sighing. "I'm so happy for you both. And now I don't have to worry about moving into an apartment in town and leaving you alone at home, Kane."

Carling felt Kane's body tense. "Holly, we've already discussed the idea of your moving into town and decided that—"

"*We* didn't discuss it. You said I couldn't and refused to discuss it any further," Holly interrupted quickly. "But that was before you got married. Things are different now. Oh, Kane, I really want to be on my own. I found a perfect little apartment in Stanton that I can move into right away. In fact, I should go as soon as possible. After all, you'll want to be alone with your bride. This is practically your honeymoon and you don't want your kid sister hanging around!''

''The house is certainly large enough to accommodate all of us,'' Kane said with a finality in his tone that Carling had come to know very well. It meant that his mind was made up and the issue wasn't open for further discussion.

Holly must have recognized it, too. She made a sound that was a cross between a groan and a wail. A tense silence settled over the car.

Carling bit her lower lip nervously. She was totally unaccustomed to sibling tension. The need to maintain a socially smooth facade was so deeply ingrained that she took a deep breath and asked politely, ''Uh, where *is* Stanton?''

''It's the nearest town, about forty miles from the ranch,'' Kane replied. ''You were sleeping when we flew over it.''

''It's small and safe and there's absolutely no reason why I shouldn't live there,'' Holly interjected bitterly. ''Except that Kane chooses to view it as the Texas version of Sodom and Gomorrah, just as he continues to see me as a dizzy teenager, who needs to be under Big Brother's constant surveillance. Carly, surely *you* can understand why—''

''Don't bother appealing to Carly for assistance, Holly,'' said Kane, as implacable as ever. ''She's never lived alone. She's twenty-eight years old and has lived with her parents all her life. And was perfectly content to do so, weren't you, sweetheart?''

Carling cleared her throat. She opened her mouth to speak, then closed it again. She wasn't about to be dragged in as a goody two-shoes role model.

''Well, that's fine for her, but not for me!'' wailed Holly. ''You expect me to live at home until I marry Joseph Wayne? Why can't you understand that I want—I *need*—some freedom and independence? I'm old enough to run my own life, Kane!''

The car braked to a sudden stop. Holly threw open the front door and jumped out of the car, crying. There was a long moment of silence.

"Well," Kane finally said, shrugging. "Welcome to the family. I'm sorry you had to be exposed to Holly's histrionics during your first fifteen minutes here at the Triple M."

Carling arched her brows thoughtfully. Apparently, relations between the McClellans weren't quite as idyllic as Kane had led her to believe. And all her sympathies lay with Holly, another apparent victim of Kane McClellan's unyielding dominance.

"It's not unusual for a twenty-two-year-old to want her own apartment," she pointed out. "You told me that Holly has graduated from college. She's of age and she's used to being on her own, so why can't she live in town if she wants to?"

"But why should she?" argued Kane. "Holly has a nice suite of rooms here, her own bedroom, bathroom and little sitting room. She'll be marrying young Joe Wayne and moving in with him soon, so why does she need a place in Stanton?"

Carling frowned. "Poor Holly. How does one explain the need for freedom and independence to a dictatorial tyrant like you? Look at it this way—your brother Scott has his own place, doesn't he? Why shouldn't Holly?"

"The circumstances are completely different. Scott works in Dallas. He *has* to live there. He can hardly commute two hundred and fifty miles to the bank each day. If Holly had a job in Stanton, it would make sense for her to live there, but she isn't interested in any employment the town has to offer. She prefers to work here on the ranch as sort of a girl Friday. She does as much or as little as she feels like on any given day. It would be absurd for her to live in Stanton."

Carling thought about that. It seemed Holly wanted to have her cake and eat it, too. She wanted a cushy job on the ranch, as well as her own place in town, which Kane would have to subsidize. When she considered the situation objectively, she realized his stance wasn't unreasonable.

But Carling wasn't in the mood to be reasonable. It was far more satisfying to view him as the implacable oppressor. "I don't think you'd find it so absurd if Holly were male. This is just another example of your overbearing sexist—"

Kane laughed slightly. "Can we skip this part of the argument if I agree that I'm a male chauvinist pig? Or whatever the current term happens to be?" He opened the car door and stepped out. Then he reached inside for Carling's hands to pull her from the car. "I don't want to fight with you, honey. I want to welcome you to your new home."

Carling blinked owlishly. The abrupt switch in topic, and in his tone and attitude as well, was disorienting. Then she saw the house and gasped. It was not the rundown, ramshackle dump she'd been dreading. Far from it. The McClellan home was a big, sprawling Spanish-style ranch house, with white stucco walls and a red-tiled roof. It was surrounded by tall trees, whose green leaves provided welcome shade from the sun. Flowering bushes and shrubs abounded and the gravel path to the long porch, which fronted the house, was lined with azalea of all colors.

Carling's jaw dropped. "It's beautiful," she said, stunned.

"I knew you'd like it." Kane smiled. "Come inside." He slipped his arm around her waist. He kept it there, chaining her to his side as he walked her to the massive front door, which was made of carved dark wood. And like a traditional bridegroom, he picked her up in his arms and carried her over the threshold.

Inside, Carling glimpsed thick white walls accented with dark walnut wood and shiny brick-colored floor tiles before Kane's lips took hers in a deep, possessive kiss. Conditioned by the long, passionate night they'd shared, her mouth opened instantly under his and she responded to him before she had time to remind herself not to.

He ended the kiss and set her on her feet just as unexpectedly as he'd picked her up. Dazed, already weak with arousal, Carling clung to him and buried her face against his chest.

She was stunned to hear cheers and a round of applause. Lifting her head, she swiftly turned around to see a line of people standing before her. They were grinning, cheering and clapping. Carling was mortified.

Incredulity followed as Kane proceeded to introduce her to his house staff. He had live-in household help? She could hardly take it all in. The Templetons' domestic help had been limited to a part-time cleaning lady. In Kane's employ were Juanita the cook, Clara and Lena, the maids, Will the gardener, Tony the jack-of-all-trades, and Marcella the housekeeper.

"You'll meet Webb Asher, the ranch manager, and the ranch hands later," Kane told her. "Webb and the hands live in bunkhouses on the property and have their own separate kitchen and mess hall. I'll take you around the spread tomorrow. Today, I want you to get acquainted with the house and the staff, especially Marcella. She'll be leaving at the end of the week. She's retiring to live near her daughter in Houston."

Marcella was petite and graying, somewhere in her late sixties or early seventies, Carling guessed, as the small woman came forward to fill her in on the housekeeping details.

"Marcella oversees the running of the house," Kane said, smiling at the older woman. "She tells Clara and Lena what housework needs to be done, works with Juanita on the weekly menus and sends Tony to the store for groceries and whatever else is needed from town. She's been with us for the past twenty years and we all consider her a member of the family," he added warmly.

"But it's good you have a wife to run your house now," Marcella said, smiling fondly from Kane to Carling. "That's as it should be."

"Come along, sweet, I'll give you a tour of the place." Kane took Carling's hand in his and guided her down the long, cool hall.

Electricity seemed to vibrate through her at the feel of his big hand engulfing hers. She was excited at the prospect of being alone with him and the reluctant admission set her teeth on edge. "I'm beginning to see why you decided to marry in such haste." Her caustic tone was the only defense she could muster. Her body had turned traitor and had begun to respond to him almost of its own volition. "Your housekeeper is retiring and you needed a replacement."

"Believe me, I could've hired twelve housekeepers at Marcella's salary for the sum I paid your father," Kane said coolly. "I thought you could take over running the house if you wanted to, but it is by no means a requirement. I can easily hire another housekeeper. I'd expected that I would have to eventually, when you're busy with our children."

Carling gaped at him. He was always one step ahead of her, keeping her off balance with unerring precision. "Children?" she repeated weakly. "I'm not even p-pregnant."

"Aren't you?" He stopped and took her by the shoulders, turning her to face him. "We haven't been using any type of birth control, Carly."

Carling blushed. Birth control had been the last thing on her mind when Kane had stirred her blood with his hot kisses and caresses. It was an additional shock to realize that the possibility of pregnancy did not fill her with horror. Rather, the thought of a baby of her own filled her with a kind of sweet, melting warmth. For the first time in her life, she imagined herself pregnant, fantasizing about the feel of a child growing in her womb, visualizing herself cuddling and feeding a soft, pink infant.

She conveniently skipped over the labor and delivery part, just as she didn't bother to dwell on the fact that her adorable, lovable baby would be Kane's child, too. Why put a damper on a perfectly delicious fantasy?

"When is your next period due?" Kane asked with his typical bluntness.

Carling blushed to the roots of her blond hair. She knew it was ridiculous to be shy with him—they'd already shared every intimacy—but she was. She stared at the gleaming tile floor, unable to look at him. "In two or three days," she mumbled.

"Looks like our timing is off this month." Kane grinned, his eyes gleaming wickedly. "But in a few weeks, you'll be in the ovulatory cycle and conception can occur—"

"Will you shut up! You're not talking about breeding cattle!"

"I like teasing you and watching you blush, Carly. You're an entertaining paradox—completely uninhibited in bed and so straitlaced out of it." He cupped her chin with his hand and leaned down to kiss her lips lightly.

After that, she was too bemused to offer any defense at all. She walked quietly with him through the house, admiring the large, spacious rooms with their Southwestern decor, the sturdy wooden furniture and Navajo rugs and earthenware ceramics perfectly complementing the stucco, wood and tile interior.

The house was cool, the air conditioning providing welcome relief from the already hot April afternoon sun. Summers, even when outside temperatures soared to unbearable highs, would be pleasant inside the house, Carling realized. She was delighted with the interior courtyard, which was filled with lush plants and a fountain with fat goldfish swimming in it.

There was even a swimming pool in the back of the house, its bright blue water shimmering in the sunlight. Cushioned chaise longues and chairs and a glass table with a striped umbrella filled the walled patio surrounding the pool, along with a variety of flowering trees and shrubs.

And she'd thought he lived in a hovel! Carling mocked herself for her earlier assumptions, and felt more than a little intimidated as well. He was very rich and very powerful while she . . . wasn't. Being here and observing the extent of his wealth drove home anew the cold, hard facts: he owned her and was in the position to determine the future of her father's career as well.

She gulped when she thought of the things she'd said to him, the way she'd behaved. Angering him was not a very good idea, Carling decided with growing apprehension. She would be helpless against the wide scope of his retaliatory wrath. Marrying him wasn't enough; she was going to have to make sure she pleased him as well. After all, a man with Kane McClellan's resources could do anything he wanted, to anybody.

"You don't have to hire another housekeeper when Marcella leaves," she said suddenly, as he led her inside from the pool area. "I can certainly run the house."

He stared at her thoughtfully. "Can you?"

"Of course. From what Marcella said, Juanita does the cooking, Clara the cleaning and Lena the laundry and ironing. My job will entail making lists and giving orders, and I happen to excel at both." She managed what she hoped was a sufficiently pleasing smile.

"And what brought on this sudden change of heart? I had the distinct impression that you saw yourself as Marcella's replacement and thoroughly resented the idea."

"Well, your distinct impression was wrong. After all, I have to do something here to—to pass the time, don't I? I live here now, I have to earn my keep."

Kane frowned. Her answer had clearly annoyed him. "You're my wife, Carly, you don't have to *earn your keep*. If you'd rather have a housekeeper to run the house, then say so. You don't have to do anything that you don't want to do."

He took her into the master bedroom suite, which was as large and luxurious as the rest of the house, perhaps even more so. Their private sitting room had its own compact disc player, large-screen color TV and VCR, just as the big family room did. The bathroom was tiled in white, green and black and had an enormous state-of-the-art Jacuzzi, along with a tile and glass shower stall, mirrored walls and triple sink.

Back in the bedroom, Carling stared at the huge oak platform bed, which was piled with pillows and covered with a colorful native woven spread. "I don't have to do anything I don't want to?" she repeated, her tongue moistening her lips. Her mouth was suddenly dry.

"Don't try to tell me that you don't want to sleep with me," Kane said, pulling her over to the edge of the bed, anticipating the remark before she could make it. "Because you do, and we both know how much."

Carling said nothing. There was an odd fear shadowing her face and he didn't like it. He couldn't understand it, either. Discounting her near virginal apprehension about sex, she'd never been frightened of him but she was unmistakably wary now. His frown deepened. He preferred her feisty and outspoken. He certainly didn't want her to hold back what she was thinking just to placate him.

"What's going on in that conniving little mind of yours?" he demanded. "This sudden capitulation of yours doesn't ring true."

"If you want me to fight with you, I will. I'll do anything you tell me to, say anything you want me to." A ghost of a smile lit her face. "We slaves aim to please. It's written in the terms of sale."

"The martyr role doesn't suit you, Carly." He pulled her into his arms and she felt him nibble sensuously along the sensitive curve of her throat. "Not that you'll be able to sustain it."

She might be a slave but she did have a modicum of pride left. "I can so," she insisted. "I'll do whatever I have to do to keep you from ruining my father's career."

His hands slipped under her sweater. "You've already done it, sweet baby. Our marriage wiped the slate clean. It's just you and me from now on."

He unclipped her bra and gently strummed over her nipples with his thumbs. Carling tried and failed to stifle a moan. "It's not that simple. We're not an equal match. You own me."

She whimpered as he inserted his thigh between hers, molding her to the hard, masculine planes of his body. Desire, primitive and insidious, was growing inside her. She wanted to cling to him as much as she wanted to fight him.

"You belong to me," Kane corrected softly. His hand smoothed over her back, then glided around to cup her breasts possessively. "There's a difference between ownership and belonging. A subtle one to be sure, but a difference all the same."

And then his mouth was on hers and he was kissing her with an ardent hunger that evoked her own wildly impassioned response. Raising the hem of her short, pleated skirt, he put his hand between her legs and the feel of his long, hard fingers against the warm, moist silk of her panties sent shock waves crashing through her.

They sank onto the bed, their bodies entwined, their breathing ragged, at the very moment that a loud, insistent knock sounded on the bedroom door.

"Kane, is Carly in there with you?" Holly called from the other side of the door. "I wanted to know if she wants to come to the barn to see the horses with me."

The abrupt cessation of passion was dizzying. Frustration, the force of which she'd never before experienced, surged through her, leaving her flushed and trembling and emotionally volatile. Carling slowly opened her eyes. She was wrapped around Kane, her body arched into his. She would have been humiliated at her obvious loss of control if she hadn't noticed that Kane didn't appear to be in any better shape than she was.

Groaning, he rolled onto his back and lay there, staring at the ceiling through slitted lids and breathing heavily, his chest visibly rising and falling. "Holly," he said through clenched teeth. "Go away."

Holly banged on the door again. "After Carly and I see the horses, I thought maybe she'd like to drive into Stanton with me and see the town." She jiggled the doorknob vigorously. "Hey, the door's locked." A giggle. "What's going on in there, anyway?"

Kane jumped off the bed. "Holly, if you don't get lost by the time I count to three—"

"No, Kane, wait." Carling sat up and placed a restraining hand on his arm. "She's just trying to be friendly. She's trying to make me feel welcome and I should—"

"She's deliberately making a pest of herself. She's set on making her presence here intolerable, so I'll be happy to pack her off to Stanton."

Carling had to concede it was an ingenious plan. But whatever Holly McClellan's motives, Carling felt obliged to offer the correct social response. She unlocked the door and opened it.

Holly stood in the hall looking quite pleased with herself. "Gee, I'm sorry if I interrupted anything," she said, grinning.

Carling tried and failed to keep from blushing. "It's— um—all right," she murmured, keeping her eyes fixed on the ground.

"No, it's not all right," Kane came up behind her and wrapped his arm around her waist, pulling her back against him. "We're going to have to lay down a few ground rules right here and now, Holly. You—"

"You're too dressed up to visit the stables, Carly," Holly put in brightly. "Why don't we do that another day? We can drive into Stanton this afternoon instead."

"Carly does not want to make the round-trip into Stanton today, Holly," Kane said tightly. "She's tired from the long flight."

Holly smiled sweetly. "Why don't we let Carly answer for herself, Kane? Are you too tired to drive into town with me, Carly?"

"I feel as if I'm caught in the cross fire here," said Carling, with an uneasy smile. Kane's arm was strong and warm against her middle. If she tilted her neck slightly, the back of her head would be resting against the solid muscular wall of his chest.

No, she didn't want to drive into Stanton, but she didn't want to reject Holly's overture of friendship, either. Vaguely, she thought that it would be a fitting revenge to leave Kane aching and frustrated in the bedroom while she flitted off to town with his little sister. Yesterday, she'd have done it in a minute. But now . . .

She was pondering this unfathomable turn of events when Kane growled, "Quit trying to stir up trouble, Holly. Carly is staying here with me. Now find yourself something to do and leave us alone."

Holly shrugged. "Well, I could drive into Stanton myself, I guess. I'm supposed to meet Joseph there for dinner, anyway. We're going to the movies later tonight, too."

"Fine. Good. Leave now and get an early start," Kane said and closed the door.

He turned to Carling. "Now where were we?"

"You were very impatient with your sister, Kane. In fact, you were downright rude. I think I should go after her and—"

"I think you should stay here, where you belong." He picked her up and carried her over to the bed, setting her on her feet to stand closely in front of him.

"Don't worry about Holly's tender feelings being bruised, she's as tough as a ranch hand." He laughed slightly. "Maybe tougher. It's a miracle that she fell in love with a quiet, sweet guy like young Joe Wayne."

"Opposites attract, so they say," Carling murmured. Of course, it was not the case between her and Kane, she assured herself.

Kane shrugged. "I'm so pleased about Holly and Joseph getting together, I try not to delve too deeply, always keeping in mind that old adage about never looking a miracle in the mouth."

She grinned in spite of herself. "I hadn't heard that one. Is it a corollary to the one about the legendary gift horse?"

It occurred to her that she and Kane were actually carrying on an amicable conversation as they stood beside the bed, about to make love. Suddenly, it was all too cozily domestic for her. After all, it wasn't as if they were a pair of congenial, infatuated newlyweds. He was a domineering, blackmailing snake and she was the property he'd purchased. Based upon that line of thinking, she was *compelled* to revive the hostilities.

"Of course you wouldn't—" she began.

"Don't." Kane cut her off immediately. "No arguing, not now."

And before she could move, speak, or even breathe, his mouth opened over hers, hot and wet and seeking. Carling felt the steely length of his arousal pressing insistently against her. Her body was melting into his, already ahead of her mind in its urgent capitulation to the passion flaring between them.

She wanted him. That is, her body certainly did, Carling amended giddily. Her rational mind certainly did not! She tried to fight the languor sweeping through her which was making her dazed and dizzy with erotic hunger. It was much too threatening to think that she—cool pragmatic Carling—was becoming emotionally involved with this autocratic, arrogant man.

But if emotions were ruled out, then her responses to him were based on pure lust and that made her nothing but a shallow, carnal creature lacking the finer, higher feelings...

The thought was appalling, even more threatening than the outrageous notion that she was falling for him. Hard. It was better not think at all. Moaning, clinging to him, she let her senses take over, banishing inhibition and intellect into the dark mists engulfing her.

Eight

Dressed in fashionable designer jeans, an apricot-colored silk blouse and a spotless pair of aerobic shoes, and with her hair neatly French-braided, Carling was ready to tour the ranch operations with Kane and Holly.

The sister and brother exchanged amused glances as she joined them in the sun-filled breakfast room. "Maybe we should go into Stanton and do a little shopping before we go near the barn—or anywhere else on the ranch," Holly suggested, grinning. "One misstep, and her clothes will be totally ruined."

"I see your point." Kane's gaze traveled lazily over Carling. "Carly, don't you have any old clothes? And a sturdy pair of boots?"

"Old clothes?" Carling repeated incredulously.

"You know—clothes that weren't purchased within the past three months. Or even the past three years." Kane gave a wry grimace. "I realize it's an alien concept to someone whose hobby and full-time occupation was shopping. What we're trying to tell you is that the clothes you're wearing aren't suitable for tramping around the barn and out on the cattle fields.''

He was definitely patronizing her! "I happen to own some old clothes," she said haughtily. "Some of my cashmere sweaters and wool suits and gowns are classic styles so I kept them. But they're still at home. I couldn't put everything I owned into your little tin plane, remember?"

Holly chuckled. Kane shrugged. "Never mind," he said, rolling his eyes heavenward. "You couldn't ride in a wool suit or a gown, anyway. Incidentally, I called a transportation company this morning and arranged to have the rest of your things shipped down here immediately, including your car. I also called your mother and she agreed to supervise the packers."

Carling was on the verge of thanking him when she remembered that he wasn't doing her any favors. If it hadn't been for his insistence upon marrying her, she wouldn't need to have her belongings shipped down here in the first place.

Instead of responding, she slipped silently into a chair and helped herself to the breakfast of freshly baked cinnamon rolls, eggs, bacon, fresh fruit, juice and coffee. She was hungry and sampled everything, surprised at the amount of food she consumed. She'd never been much of a breakfast eater, preferring only half a piece of toast and a cup of coffee or tea in the morning. But then, she'd never spent her nights the way she'd spent last night, her second one as Mrs. Kane McClellan....

As she reveled in the memories of the night before, her hand shook and coffee sloshed over the rim of the cup.

"Okay, we'll go to Stanton and buy a pair of boots, a hat and a more practical shirt and pair of jeans," Kane's voice cut in on her reverie. "But, Carly, we don't go shopping every day around here," he added in a tone which set her teeth on edge. "I don't believe in running up big monthly bills on charge accounts. Here at the Triple M, shopping is for provisions, not a way of life. We buy things we need when we need them, but—''

''Yessir, life is tough here at the Triple M State Prison,'' Holly interjected dryly. ''We inmates are only allowed out of our cells to work the ranch and we get a couple bucks a week to spend at the cell block canteen. Don't expect to do anything but hard time here, Carly.''

Kane frowned reprovingly. ''Stay out of this, Holly.''

''On the contrary, I appreciate her filling me in on the rules and regulations, Warden,'' Carling said coolly. ''Of course, I realize that she's not a lifer here, so she has certain privileges that I could never hope to have. For example, I don't expect you to spend a cent on me. I'll make use of whatever I already have. You'll *never* have to worry about me running up bills by spending your precious money!''

She tossed down her napkin and would have stormed from the table if Kane hadn't seized her arm. ''Sit back down,'' he ordered. ''You've deliberately chosen to misinterpret everything I said.''

''I didn't have to misinterpret anything. You spelled it all out quite clearly,'' Carling said tightly, trying to wriggle away from him. ''You think I'm an irresponsible, extravagant spendthrift who will blithely run you into bankruptcy.''

A sudden hot flood of tears burned her eyes. Good Lord, wasn't that what she and her mother had almost done to her father? The insight was shattering.

Kane saw the haunted look shadow her face and almost cursed aloud. He could guess what she was thinking, some nonsense about being responsible for her father's financial woes when the senator's own pride and fiscal foolishness was the cause of that mess.

He stared at her thoughtfully. He'd never been renowned for his sensitivity, far from it. But he was beginning to understand Carling in a way he would have never thought himself capable. He'd quickly become attuned to her, to her emotions and her moods...

His body began to tighten. It was incredible, impossible, after their fevered coming together last night and their slow, languid early-morning passion just a few hours ago, but he was starting to want her again.

He thought of his plans, marrying her and bringing her here to share his home and raise a family. It had been such a convenient and practical idea, sparing him all the time and effort of a stupid courtship which might not have ended in the marriage he'd wanted anyway. But something had gone awry. His feelings for his bride were anything but convenient or practical; they were raging, ferocious. She was swiftly becoming an obsession.

And she professed to despise him. Actually, she had every right to. He had barged into her life and irrevocably changed it, completely against her will. Kane frowned. This would never do. Second-guessing himself was wildly out of character for him. He'd never been plagued by ruminations and self-doubt; he did what he felt was right and was invariably proven correct. Pushing aside his troubling thoughts, he resorted to action, his usual panacea.

"We're going into Stanton, Carly," he said decisively. "I'll buy you the clothes you need."

"I'll buy them myself!" Carling snapped. "I have my own money with me."

"I said I'll buy them and I will. The fifty dollars you have in your wallet won't even buy one boot, let alone a pair of them, not to mention a Lady Stetson and a few pairs of jeans and shirts."

"How do you know how much money I have in my wallet?" demanded Carling.

"I looked," he replied without the slightest trace of an apology.

"You went into my purse?" Carling was incensed. "You had no right, that's a blatant invasion of privacy."

"There is no reason for secrecy between us, Carly," he said tautly. "Not now, not ever."

"Privacy isn't the same as secrecy, you—you block-head!" Carling cried.

"You two have an interesting marriage," Holly remarked, and the couple turned, startled, to face her. Both had completely forgotten her presence.

Holly smiled devilishly. "Yeah, I'm still here. And since you two are so fascinating to observe, you can be sure that I'll *always* be around. Don't count on any privacy *or* secrecy as long as I'm living in this house." She left the table, humming.

Carling and Kane stared at each other, nonplussed. And then Carling's lips curved into an irrepressible smile. "So this is what it's like to have a little sister?" She laughed in spite of her determination to stay angry. Somehow, her indignant rage had dissipated. "And to think I desperately wanted one for years!"

"Yeah, well," Kane rubbed the nape of his neck with his hand. "You know what they say...be careful what you wish for—"

"Because you may get it," they chorused. Their gazes met and held.

Then Kane rose from his chair and held out his hand to her. "Let's go into town, Carly," he said quietly.

Carling gazed at him, feeling suddenly breathless. Standing there, so commandingly masculine, so virile and strong, he was more attractive than any man she'd ever known. Her pulse began to race and her legs felt wobbly. She'd never simply *looked* at a man and felt this yearning, this temptation to forget about everything but him and the way he made her feel.

She gave her head a shake, as if to clear it. This would never do. He was beginning to dominate her thoughts as well as her body and her life. She couldn't let it happen. "I don't want any new clothes," she said, her voice as frozen as an ice floe. "I'll take my chances with these, thank you all the same."

"You'll go with me and wear what I buy you, thank you all the same," Kane mimicked rudely. He scooped her up in his arms and stalked across the room, down the hall and out the front door.

He was ready to deposit her into the front seat of the station wagon, when they were approached by a darkly tanned, blond man with a tall rangy build and startlingly green eyes. He was the quintessential cowboy, from his wide-brimmed hat to his dusty boots. "Kane, I understand you got married. Is this the new missus?" he drawled.

"She is." Kane turned around so the other man could get a better look at Carling.

Why, he was inspecting her—and Kane was showing her off—as if she were some prized piece of livestock! Carling seethed at the unspoken, mutual machismo going on here. "Put me down," she ordered Kane.

He didn't, of course, so she was introduced to Webb Asher, the ranch manager, while being held high against Kane's chest.

"Let me get the door for you," Webb said with exaggerated politeness, flinging open the front door of the station wagon.

Kane put Carling inside. "We're heading into Stanton," he said to Webb. "Don't expect us back at any particular time."

"Right." Webb nodded. "It was a pleasure to meet you, Mrs. McClellan," he added with a smile that Carling found insolent.

"I don't like your ranch manager," she announced, as Kane steered the station wagon away from the house.

"You don't have to like him. He does a helluva job and that's all that matters."

She folded her arms across her chest and scowled. "I don't like you, either," she added, throwing down the gauntlet.

Kane did not pick it up. "Yes, you do. It's killing you, but you're liking me more and more, Carly."

What could she say to that? His confidence was virtually unshakable. No, she corrected herself. It wasn't confidence, it was arrogance, damnable, detestable arrogance. Because she still couldn't come up with a suitably scathing reply, his invitation to find a station on the radio was a welcome diversion. They listened to her favorite music all the way into Stanton.

Stanton, Texas, was a small town, but not as small as Carling had been expecting—and dreading. There was a two-block shopping district where most all necessities—and even some luxuries—could be purchased. There was a movie theater, several bars, a small hotel and a family-style restaurant. One of the ubiquitous fast-food chains had a franchise there as well.

Kane took her on a brief driving tour of the town, pointing out the churches, the post office, the library and the two schools, Stanton Elementary for kindergarten through eighth grade and the four-year Stanton High.

"Our kids will go there," he said casually, as if it were the most natural thing in the world for them to be discussing their future offsprings' education. "A school bus will pick them up and drop them off at the end of the road leading to the house."

"It's a long commute, especially for small children," Carling said witheringly, not wanting to foster the illusion of compatibility in any way. Bad enough that the drive into town had been completed without an argument or cross word, now he wanted to prolong the period of peace.

"It's an easy trip," replied Kane. "The road is straight and flat, and you saw how little traffic there is on the highway between the Triple M and Stanton. The school bus makes good time."

Carling arched her brows. "So in addition to sending little children to a school forty miles from home, there is the added danger of a speed demon bus driver who is determined to make 'good time.'"

Kane laughed. "You're very quick," he said approvingly. "You're always ready with a good comeback."

He thought she was teasing him, just kidding around to make him laugh! Carling was nonplussed. Should she tell him that she wasn't, that she'd intended to fire the opening salvo in the resumption of their own private war? Somehow, an explanation seemed laborious and beside the point, like trying to explain a joke to someone who didn't get it.

She glanced at him. He was still grinning. More disconcerting was the involuntary smile beginning to twist the corners of her own mouth. It was difficult to stay angry at someone who thought you were witty and entertaining. He'd said she was quick, always ready with a good comeback.

Wouldn't some of her less-than-enthusiastic former dates be surprised to hear that description of her? They'd described her as cold, starchy and humorless—to her face. Her feelings had been terribly hurt, but she'd never let them know....

Kane bought her the practical clothes, boots and hat, and she politely thanked him, promising herself that these were the first, last and only things he would ever buy for her. She might be a slave, but she was a proud one, she reminded herself. And though her father had managed to garner a chunk of the McClellan fortune, she would not attempt to follow suit, even if it meant never shopping again!

Spring roundup was in full swing at the Triple M, and the calves were culled, branded and separated by the cowboys under the supervision of the ranch manager. Carling watched as hundreds of calves were vetted into a chuted corral with gates opening into neat paddocks where they were branded. It was noisy and dusty, with cowboys shouting and calves bawling.

Carling shuddered. She found the whole process extremely distressing. "I feel so sorry for them," she said, staring anxiously at the scene. "First dragged away from their mothers and then hurt with that hot branding iron.

Can't they at least be given a local anesthetic before they'r
branded?''

Kane, Holly, and Webb found her comment hilarious an
howled with laughter. Carling walked away from them an
climbed into the pickup truck, where she waited for Kan
and Holly to join her.

"We have over one hundred thousand head of cattle o
the Triple M," Holly said proudly as Kane drove the truc
away from the corral. "Kane has a computer in his offic
with records on each one and Webb is the best ranch man
ager in the county, maybe even the whole state."

Carling had already visited Kane's office, which was lo
cated in the house. A big, antique mahogany desk share
space with all kinds of modern electronic equipment, an in
congruous combination she'd found amusing. He was a
much businessman as rancher, she'd learned, when h
mentioned his other investments, stocks, bonds, oil leasin
and real estate holdings, which comprised the McClella
wealth.

"The key is diversity," he'd explained, pulling her dow
onto his lap.

Remembering what had happened next brought a flush o
color to her cheeks. The man was not only creative in mon
etary matters, he was also incredibly creative when it cam
to making love. Carling knew she would never be able t
look at his wide, polished desk without remembering tha
late afternoon interlude they'd shared.

"You'll like visiting the stable," said Kane, his voic
breaking into her intimate recollections. "We have severa
newborn foals that—"

"You're not going to brand *them* too, I hope?" she asked
archly.

He shot her an amused glance. "No, honey, we don'
brand pure-blooded Arabian horses." He and Holly ex
changed wide grins.

Carling smiled politely and pretended to understand th
ranch humor they were enjoying. She was not looking for

ward to visiting the horses, not even the baby ones. Once in the barn, someone was bound to assume that she was dying to ride one of the horses and then make the suggestion. In truth, Carling had absolutely no desire to ride a horse. She'd managed to postpone the dreaded visit to the stables her entire first week on the ranch.

But now the moment was at hand, and she dutifully admired Kane's prize Arabian stallions, though she privately found them wild-eyed and terrifying. She exclaimed over the foals as they suckled their mothers, but she preferred the young barn cats who chased each other through the wood chips that littered the floor. They were small and close to the ground, unlike the horses who seemed to tower above it.

Inevitably, Kane and Holly eagerly offered to saddle up one of the quarter horses for her to ride, a sturdy, frisky mare called Lady Slipper.

Carling eyed Lady Slipper, who seemed to stare back at her with a fiendish glee. "I'd better get back to the house," she said quickly. "I told Juanita that I'd look over the menus and write up the grocery list."

"That can wait," Kane was already saddling his own mount. "The horses need to be exercised. We haven't ridden together since you came to the ranch, Carly."

"There's a reason for that," Carling mumbled.

Holly was already on her horse, which whinnied spiritedly and kicked up its hooves in anticipation of leaving the barn. Carling's heart leaped into her throat. She watched Kane lead the prancing Lady Slipper toward her and she began to slowly back away. "I'm not going to ride," she announced.

"Of course you are," Kane countered calmly.

He assumed she was being contrary simply to rile him, Carling realized anxiously. Hardly an unusual course of action for her, but this time she wasn't trying to annoy him. She was trying to save her life!

"Let me put it another way. If you want to get me on that horse, you're going to have to knock me unconscious and tie me to the saddle." Lady Slipper gave a snort and Carling's eyes widened. "She knows I don't like her and she doesn't like me, either," she added nervously. "Take her back and let me go to the house."

"You don't ride?" Holly appeared thunderstruck. "You don't like horses?"

"I had a bad experience with a horse once," Carling said, her eyes fixed on Lady Slipper, who never seemed to stop moving. The young horse was the essence of animal strength and power, one Carling knew she couldn't hope to control. Her stomach churned with anxiety. "When I was six, my father and I went to a rodeo rally fund-raiser and someone put me up on this gigantic horse. It was jittery from the noise of the crowd, and it started to buck. It threw me off. I broke my collarbone and my arm and had a serious concussion. I saw double for days and was in the hospital for two weeks."

"Wow!" Holly was clearly impressed. "I've been thrown lots of times, but I was never hurt badly enough to be taken to the hospital."

"You can see why I've avoided horses ever since," Carling concluded. She turned to Kane to find him watching her intently.

"You tried something once, it turned out badly and you made a vow to never do it again," he drawled. "That whole scenario has a familiar ring to it."

Carling's breath caught in her throat and she had to gasp for air. He was alluding to her attitude toward sex! Until he'd come along and changed it completely, that is. "There is no similarity whatsoever," she insisted.

"Isn't there?"

"No!"

"I think there is. And we both know what happened when I insisted that you break your mule-headed vow of abstinence, don't we, Carly? The same rules apply here."

"What are you talking about?" Holly demanded.

"This is a private conversation that doesn't concern you, Holly," Kane said, exasperated. "Kindly make yourself scarce."

"It might not concern me, but it interests me," Holly shot back. "And if I had my own place in Stanton, I wouldn't be here invading your privacy. Right, Carly?" She turned to her sister-in-law for confirmation.

"That's right," Carling agreed succinctly. "And I'm not going to let you bully me into riding that horse, Kane McClellan. It wants to kill me, I can see it in her eyes and—"

Kane laughed. "I concede that Lady Slipper is a bit too frisky for a beginner. We'll start with good old Lucky Charm. Get down and saddle her up, Holly."

"No, don't, Holly," countered Carling. "I don't care if old Lucky Charm has one shoe in the glue factory, I'm not riding her. I refuse to get on any horse and no one is going to make me." Straightening her shoulders, she stalked determinedly toward the house.

She turned her head at the sound of prancing hooves. Holly had ridden up alongside her. "He's taking Lady Slipper back into the stable," Holly exclaimed. "Looks like you won this round, Carly. I can hardly believe it—nobody says no to Kane and makes it stick."

"Well, there has to be a first time for everything," Carling said with satisfaction. "Enjoy your ride, Holly."

"I will. I just wish that . . ." The girl's voice trailed off as a thunder of hooves sounded from behind them. "Uh-oh! Looks like you're going riding after all, Carly."

Carling saw the huge, chestnut-colored horse with Kane astride, heading toward them. She wanted to scream and run, but she resisted the impulse. She should have guessed that saying no to an aggressive male like Kane had presented him with an irresistible challenge. Well, she wouldn't back down. She would stand her ground and state her case reasonably and rationally.

Kane slowed the horse to a trot and reined in beside her. "There's nothing to be afraid of, Carly," he promised in soothing tones. "I'm going to put you up on the horse with me, just to get the feel of it. You'll be perfectly safe."

"Kane, I've already explained why I—"

"I want you to learn to ride, Carly."

"But why? It's possible to live a rich, full life without getting onto the back of a horse, you know."

"When you live on a ranch with a subspecialty in horse breeding, you have to know at least the rudiments of riding."

"You make it sound like a law or a religious obligation or something. That's ridiculous! Forget it, Kane."

"Sorry, honey." He didn't sound sorry at all as he suddenly bent down to grab her and pull her up to sit on the saddle in front of him. "You're going to enjoy riding, Carly. I guarantee you'll thank me for this."

Carling clutched the pommel with both hands. She was balanced precariously between Kane and the front of the saddle. The ground seemed miles below them and the excited horse was making all kinds of alarming movements. This time she *did* follow her instincts. She shrieked.

"I'm going to fall off!"

"No, you're not. Sit still," Kane ordered roughly. He had one hand on the reins to control the horse while he wrapped his other arm around Carling's waist to control her frantic wriggling. Neither effort succeeded very well.

"Let her down, Kane. She's scared to death!" Holly shouted.

The high-strung horse required gentle handling, and when Carling's struggles made Kane accidentally jerk hard on the reins, the animal panicked. It bucked and reared like an unbroken bronco in a Wild West show. Kane, who'd successfully ridden unbroken broncos before, managed to hang on, but there was no way he could keep a terrified novice like Carling in the saddle when her violent struggling thwarted his every attempt to do so.

Moments later, she fell from the horse, hitting the ground with a thud. Holly screamed and Kane's horse became even wilder. It took all his strength to keep the animal from trampling Carling's inert form. After he'd guided it safely away from her, he quickly dismounted and slapped the horse's rear, sending it dashing toward the barn.

"Carly!" He raced over to her, a sickening combination of horror and terror surging through him. The accident replayed crazily in his head and once again he could feel her slip from his grasp, see her fall from the horse and hear the hard force with which she'd struck the ground. Then came the added nightmare of the horse kicking dangerously near her, of watching her lying in the dust, so still. So very still.

Holly was already crouched over Carling when he knelt down beside her. "Oh, Kane!" was all his sister could exclaim in dismay. "Oh, Kane!"

He filled in the unspoken part. How could you let this happen? How could you do this to her? She'd been terrified of horses and he'd forced her onto one. "It's all my fault," he said thickly. He felt as though he'd been kicked in the gut. He couldn't swallow, couldn't breathe.

"You're damn right it is," Carling muttered darkly.

"She's conscious!" squealed Holly. "Oh, thank God! Carly, can you hear me? Do you know where you are?"

"Of course. I never lost consciousness." Slowly, gingerly, Carling raised herself to a sitting position. "I landed on my stomach and had the wind knocked out of me, so I couldn't breathe. Believe me, you don't feel like moving or speaking if you can't breathe."

"She's okay!" cried Holly exultantly. "She sounds just like her old self!"

Kane, pale and shaken, immediately began to run his hands over Carling's body. "Can you move your arms? Your legs?" His voice was hoarse. "Are you in pain?" His fingers examined her head, her neck. "Do you—see double?"

Carling stared at him. No, she was not seeing double; there was only one of Kane and he looked distraught. His face was white and his hands were shaking. *Kane McClellan!* It was amazing to see him in such a rattled state.

"Carling, I'm so sorry."

He'd actually said her name correctly. Carling gazed at him, perplexed. Surprisingly, it didn't sound right, coming from him. She'd gotten used to his nickname.

"I'm going to carry you to the car and drive to the airstrip," Kane continued. He looked and sounded positively shattered. "We'll fly into Dallas immediately and have you seen at Parkland Memorial Hospital."

"The hospital in Dallas?" Carling said incredulously. Since she'd hit the ground with a solid wallop, she would probably have some bruises. It certainly hadn't been pleasant to lie stunned and breathless for those first few moments. But she knew she wasn't badly hurt.

"I'm all right. I don't even need to see a doctor, let alone go to a hospital," she declared.

Kane picked her up and strode toward the house with lightning speed. "Sweetheart, I know you're being brave. I'll make this up to you, I promise. After you get out of the hospital, I'll take you anywhere you want to go. If you want to visit your parents in Washington, we'll fly up there, commercial, first-class, if you want and—"

"Kane, I'm all right. I don't need a doctor. And if you don't put me down right this minute, I—I'm going to scream."

To her astonishment, he set her on her feet immediately. When had such a paltry threat ever worked with Kane? But he looked terrible, tormented.

"Carly, I never wanted you to get hurt," he said.

It came as a distinct shock to her that she didn't like seeing him this way. Gone was his unflappable confidence and maddening arrogance. He thought she was hurt and he blamed himself. At this point, *he* was hurting more than she was.

"You think you know what's right for everyone," she began.

He flinched. For reasons she didn't even want to think about, the stricken look on his face affected her.

"I know you didn't mean for me to fall," she said quietly. "But I'm okay." Hesitantly, she reached out her hand and laid it on his forearm. "Honestly, I am. It was an accident, it's over and let's just forget about it."

He covered her hand with his. "When I saw you on the ground—" He took a deep breath and swallowed hard.

"The accident wasn't your fault, Kane, but I really am afraid of horses."

He pulled her into his arms and hugged her hard. Carling let him, not even objecting to the pressure on her bruised rib cage. She was aware that some invisible, intangible line had been crossed, but she didn't want to dwell on what it all meant.

"You never have to go near a horse again if you don't want to," Kane promised fervently. "I promise I'll never again suggest that you ride."

He knew it was a most un-Kane-like declaration, but he wasn't feeling at all like his normal self. Despite Carling's generous disclaimers, he knew he'd helped cause the accident. That she was unhurt didn't lessen the seriousness of what he'd done. He had made the decision for her to ride, certain that it was right because he'd come to believe that he inevitably made the right choices, for himself and everyone else.

But this time he'd been wrong! He'd always had difficulty in admitting he was wrong. Since his parents' deaths when he'd taken over the ranch and began to build the McClellan fortune, when he'd assumed guardianship of the kids, he'd abandoned the notion that he ever could be wrong. He didn't dare be wrong, not with so much depending upon him.

But he'd definitely been wrong this time and Carling had paid the price. He never should have pulled her onto that horse. He had been arrogant and blindly stupid. Carling could have been critically injured or killed. He gazed down at the warm, vital woman he held in his arms and thought what his life would be like without her. The prospect was infinitely chilling, much harder to bear than the revelation that he was not infallible.

She'd been his wife for ten days, but he couldn't seem to remember life without her. Now he couldn't even envision a life without her. It worried him that she should have so much power over him. No woman ever had before. And it was a relentless, all-consuming power, so much more than the sexual power of a desirable woman. He'd begun to suspect that his feelings for her went far beyond sex. Today's incident confirmed that suspicion.

They were a quiet, reflective pair as they walked slowly toward the house, his arm around her shoulders.

"About the trip to Washington to visit your parents," he said, as they entered the house.

"The one where I fly commercial, first-class, instead of in your toy airplane?" Carling's blue eyes sparkled mischievously. "Let me guess—the offer has been rescinded."

"No, no, of course not!" Kane hastened to reassure her. "I wanted to know when you wanted to go so that I could make the reservations."

Carling considered it. Back to Washington. Home to Mama and Daddy. Lunch and shopping with the girls, lunch and shopping with Mama, lunch and entertaining, visiting constituents and colleagues with Daddy. Dinner with whomever happened to be available.

She frowned thoughtfully. Somehow, her former life had lost some of its allure. The thought of shopping particularly palled when she considered the state of the Templeton finances.

"I guess I'll stay here," she said, carefully avoiding Kane's eyes, not wanting to give away... what? She wasn't sure. "All my things are due to arrive here any day now and

I ought to be around to unpack. It seems a bit foolish to go home when all my stuff will be here.''

''*This* is your home, Carly,'' Kane corrected with a definite, dogmatic trace of his usual self. ''Your parents' place is your former home.''

To their mutual amazement, she didn't deny it.

Nine

———

The middle of May was warm and sunny and free of the high humidity that would later make the summer months so sticky and oppressive. Carling took advantage of the pleasant weather and slipped outside to the pool after she'd organized the house and staff for the day.

Her swimsuit was a one-piece, modestly cut, black and strapless, with a white ruffle across the top. It was a suit that would draw complimentary glances from women without inspiring lust in their husbands and sons. Always aware of her role as a senator's daughter, Carling had always chosen such suits.

It wasn't until she'd come to the ranch that she had even thought of wearing something like the peacock-blue string bikini she'd seen in one of the mail-order catalogs that were delivered to the house. She allowed her mind to drift, visualizing herself in that same bikini, sunning herself by the pool...

She would be drowsy, lulled into sleepiness by the warmth of the sun, and wouldn't hear Kane approach. He would tell her that she needed to apply more sunscreen, that she was so fair-skinned that she must take extra precautions against sunburn. He would have the lotion with him, of course, and would begin to apply it, with long, slow, sweeping strokes. She would feel herself becoming aroused, feel her nipples tighten to pebble hardness, feel the syrupy warmth between her thighs. She would try to lie still, try to disguise her arousal, but Kane would know. He would continue to tease her, not touching her where she wanted to be touched until she was moving sinuously beneath his hands, until she was flushed and moaning and out of control. She would unclip the bikini top and cast it to the ground and Kane would look at her, with that sexy, hungry smile on his face . . .

Carling's book slipped through her fingers and hit her foot. The jolt of pain catapulted her out of her daydream into full awareness. She glanced furtively around her, embarrassed by how completely she'd been involved in the fantasy. She'd never had a sexual fantasy in her life, until she'd married Kane, and now . . .

Carling pressed her hands to her hot cheeks to cool them. Now when she wasn't making love with Kane, she was daydreaming about it. She waited half-expectantly for the wave of rage and shame that should follow this confession. After all, he'd bought her, practically kidnapped her, for heaven's sake, and if she had any pride, she should continue to protest her enslavement and diabolically plan his downfall.

Though she couldn't seem to work herself into a full-fledged vengeful fury, Carling did manage to achieve a state of righteous indignation.

Scowling, she stretched out on the yellow-and-white chaise longue and opened her book, a thick historical romance that Holly had highly recommended. By page five the heroine had been kidnapped by a lusty pirate captain who, to her, bore a startling physical resemblance to Kane. By page fifteen, the heroine was in the hero's bed helplessly succumbing to his virile charms—and Carling was no longer scowling.

Lena, the maid, appeared on the patio in the middle of a particularly intense scene on page seventeen, to announce the arrival of a visitor, Edie Wayne, from the neighboring Wayne ranch. Carling sighed inwardly and closed her book.

"Carly, my dear, it's wonderful to meet you! I've heard so much about you from my son Joseph!" Edie Wayne greeted Carling effusively, giving her an affectionate hug. "I was delighted to hear about Kane's marriage and I had to restrain myself from coming over any earlier. I know how newlyweds value their privacy!"

Carling smiled. She was pleased that she didn't blush. These days mere references to sexuality didn't make her lose her cool. "I'm delighted to meet you too, Edie. I understand your Joseph and Kane's sister Holly are—"

"Oh yes, Joey and Holly! Such an inseparable pair!" Edie shook her head in a gesture of maternal indulgence. "You must be sick of seeing that son of mine around here every evening. I tried to explain to *him* about newlyweds and privacy but he's too wrapped up in Holly to think of anything else. You've been very kind to invite him to dinner so many times. Why, he hasn't spent an evening at home in weeks!"

Carling was silent. Maybe she hadn't heard right. Had she had too much sun? She'd never even met Joseph Wayne, much less invited him to dinner. Holly mentioned his name frequently and she was forever driving to the Wayne ranch to have dinner and spend the evening with him there or meeting him in town.

Except that Joseph Wayne's mother said that her son hadn't spent an evening at home in weeks. Carling chewed her lower lip thoughtfully. She'd never had a younger sister but she recognized a masterful piece of sibling deception going on here. Kane thought his little sister was visiting the Waynes and the Waynes thought their son was visiting the McClellans.

Loyalty to Holly kept her silent on the subject of the couple's alleged whereabouts. She and Edie Wayne sipped tall, cool glasses of lemonade and chatted. When Edie mentioned that she would like to throw a big party to welcome Carling to the county and to celebrate the McClellans' marriage, Carling was delighted and immediately agreed. She wanted to meet her neighbors and although she hadn't missed the intensive socializing of her past, she was ready to enjoy a big, friendly party.

"There is one problem though, my dear," Edie said, frowning a little. "If you tell Kane we're having a party, he won't come. He hates them."

Carling thought of the tales of the reclusive rancher she'd heard before she had ever met Kane; then she remembered how much he'd enjoyed their wedding reception—not at all. She nodded. "I see you know him well."

"Everybody who knows him thinks the world of Kane so he's always invited to everything, though he rarely comes." Edie paused, then brightened. "Suppose we engage in a little creative deception? You could tell Kane that I invited just the two of you over for dinner next Saturday. Oh, and tell him that Holly and Joseph will be there, too. Kane enjoys very small gatherings and he's as enthused about the kids' romance as my husband and I. I'm sure he'll come."

"Yes, I'm sure he will," Carling agreed. Kane was extraordinarily pleased with Holly's romance with young Joe Wayne and he was eagerly anticipating their wedding.

Edie Wayne left shortly afterward and Carling turned to page seventeen of her book. She'd read two paragraphs when Holly, slim and lithe in a lime green swimsuit, bounded out onto the deck.

"Kane'll be out in a few minutes," Holly announced. "He's changing into his suit."

Carling's heart did a funny little somersault. The mere mention of Kane's name could create that effect. She was exhibiting a lot of peculiar signs and symptoms these days: like not being able to take her eyes off him when he was in a room with her, like hanging on his every word, like thinking of him when she was alone and starting to ache for his kiss, to throb and burn for his ardent caresses. Squirming and shifting her legs, she was starting to feel that way now.

Both to divert herself and also to satisfy her curiosity, she turned her attention to Holly. "Edie Wayne came by today to invite us to a party. Kane thinks it's just us and the Waynes, but Edie plans to invite everybody they know who knows Kane."

Holly chuckled. "Kane will hate that." She paused. "Did—uh—Edie happen to mention Joseph?"

"She thanked me for having him over to dinner all these weeks. She remarked how inseparable you two are, how he spends all his time over here and is seldom home in the evenings."

Holly sank into the chair beside Carling. "Did you tell her—otherwise?"

"That you've been telling us that you spend most of your evenings over there? No, I didn't."

Holly let out a heartfelt sigh of relief. "Oh, thanks, Carly. I owe you one, a big one!"

"Then I'd like to call it in now, Holly. What's going on? Why did you lie, to the Waynes and to Kane and me? Where are you and Joseph really spending your time?"

Holly blushed fiercely. "Oh, Carly, please don't ask me that!"

And then Carling understood. As someone who'd only recently become involved in an intense sexual relationship, she recognized the young woman's constraint. Holly's neighbor-boyfriend was also her lover and since both lived at home with their families, they were meeting in clandestine places. But where? she wondered. The small hotel in Stanton? The barn? The field? The back seat of a car?

Carling shuddered. No wonder she had been such a poor candidate for an affair. All of the aforementioned places struck her as either embarrassing, uncomfortable or inconvenient. Or all three!

"I'm not going to press you for details, Holly," she said soothingly. "But maybe you and Joseph should think of getting married sooner rather than later? If you had your own place and your own—" she cleared her throat "—bed, you wouldn't have to—" she lowered her eyes discreetly "—go searching for—um—privacy."

"Yeah, sure." Holly giggled nervously. "Thanks a lot for understanding, Carly. You're a terrific sis!" She raced to the edge of the pool, dived gracefully into the water and began to swim laps.

It went without saying that Carling wouldn't mention this little talk to Kane. Anyway, she didn't want to be the one to tell him that his little sister was sneaking around having sex. She knew Kane well enough to know that would truly rankle, no matter how much he liked Joseph and the Waynes.

Kane joined her a few minutes later, wearing black swim trunks. His chest was bare, his legs long and muscular. Even his walk was sexy and pure male. The sparks, which had been kindled by her earlier thoughts of him, burst into a full blaze.

She wanted him. Her body tightened in anticipation and delicious shivers tingled through her. She was no longer the inhibited young woman she had been just six and a half weeks ago. Kane had released the passionate woman within her, introducing her to the pleasures of her own burgeoning sexuality.

"I thought you had some business in your office to attend to," she said, trying to sound nonchalant. But her pulse was racing and there was a buttery warmth seeping through her limbs.

"I took care of it. Made a few calls to Dallas and to New York. Now I'm free." He smiled, a rather dangerous, predatory smile which stirred her senses.

"See you two later!" Holly shouted, as she climbed from the pool and headed into the house. "I'm having dinner at Joseph's tonight. Don't expect me back till late."

"Holly is being considerate and letting us alone?" Kane said mockingly. "I can hardly believe it. Maybe she's finally given up on the idea of moving into Stanton."

Carling was surprised by how much she wanted to tell him the truth. Keeping secrets from Kane didn't feel right. But wasn't Holly entitled to her privacy? She was an adult, capable of making her own choices and decisions. And there were some things that a young woman might feel uncomfortable sharing with an overprotective older brother, her sex life being one of them. Though brotherless herself, Carling could certainly understand that.

Kane traced his finger along the smooth skin just above the white ruffle of Carling's swimsuit. "You're very fair. You have to be very careful in the sun to avoid a bad burn."

Carling's eyes swept over her demure suit and she wished she'd ordered that outrageous peacock-blue string bikini. "Are you going to insist on putting more sunscreen on me?" she asked huskily, gazing at him from beneath lowered lashes.

"Later. After we've had a swim." Unexpectedly, he caught both her hands in his and jerked her to her feet. "Let's go. Last one into the water has to—"

"I don't want to go into the water. I'll get wet."

"Water will make you wet. An interesting theory," Kane said drolly. He picked her up in his arms and strode purposefully to the pool. "Let's test it out right now."

He was going to drop her in the water! "Kane, don't!" she squealed.

He ignored her, walking to the deep end of the pool and teasingly swinging her over the water. "One—two—"

"Kane, please listen! If you're going to throw me in, at least do it in the shallow end. I—I can't swim!"

Kane's game came to an abrupt stop. He immediately set her on her feet. "You can't swim?" he echoed incredulously.

"I fell into a neighbor's pool when I was four years old. By the time someone noticed me, I was already on the bottom and had to be revived. Mama and Daddy were hysterical—they wouldn't let me near water again.''

Kane groaned. "You're too smart not to see the pattern here, Carly. I'm not going to force you into the water, but I think you should try to overcome your fear of it and learn to swim. You're not a scared little girl anymore. You're an adult. We have a pool here, we'll have children who will be using it and—''

"I'm not afraid of the water. I haven't been for years,'' she interjected swiftly. She didn't want him to think she was a hopeless phobic! "I wanted to learn to swim, especially when I was a teenager, but by then all my friends already knew how and I felt stupid admitting that I didn't. So I would always say that I didn't want to go into the water because I didn't want to get my hair wet.''

"And no teenage boy ever took that as a challenge and tried to toss you into the pool anyway?''

Carling smiled wryly. "No. Not a single one dared.''

"Even as a teen, the Ice Princess could freeze a guy at twenty paces?''

"Oh yes.''

"It's a good thing I wasn't around then.'' He smiled a daring, challenging smile. "You know what I would have done to you, don't you?''

"Made me go into the water despite my protests, telling me that it would be good for me? That I needed it? That I'd feel more content and calm after I'd worked off all my high-strung energy... in the pool?''

Her smiles, her words were deliberately provocative. So was the tilt of her head and the subtle thrust of her hips. The Carling of six weeks ago would have been shocked at her own brazenness, the Carling of today reveled in it.

Kane's eyes swept over her and he growled softly, "Oh baby, you're asking for it.''

"Somewhat of a cliché, but still a perfect cue.'' Carling laughed seductively. "What else can I say but, 'Am I going to get it?' ''

Tension vibrated between them, but there was also genuine warmth and affection in his eyes and in hers as he reached for her. "Most definitely, honey. Right here. Right now." He picked her up again.

"In the water?" she asked with languid interest.

"That's a more advanced course. You'll take it later." He laid her down on the chaise longue and lowered the bodice of her swimsuit. The sight of her breasts, so white and soft and beautifully shaped, peaked with taut pink nipples stirred his blood. He knew he would never tire of looking at her, never stop wanting her. Had he not been half-drunk with desire, the thought might have worried him as bordering on the obsessive.

But when he took her nipple in his mouth, she arched and cried out, holding his head close, stroking his nape, his hair with her slender fingers, Kane could think of nothing but how good it felt to hold her, to taste her, to pleasure her.

He sucked first one breast, then the other until Carling was writhing and twisting and shuddering for release. She wanted him now, deep inside her; an empty throb ached between her thighs. Insistently she pressed herself against the muscular column of his hair-roughened thigh.

"Kane, please," she gasped. Her hands slipped inside the waistband of his swim trunks and she found him, smooth and hard and pulsing with virile strength.

"Yes, baby. Yes, love," he muttered hoarsely and helped her pull off his suit.

When he tried to remove hers, the tight spandex material seemed to cling to her like a second skin. He pulled and tugged, his usual dexterity impeded by the consuming force of his desire. "Is this thing glued on or what?" he gasped with exasperation.

Carling joined the struggle. Why hadn't she ever realized how ridiculously impossible it was to get out of this suit? She felt like a fat lady struggling out of a too-tight girdle, hardly an alluring image!

When they'd finally worked the suit off, Kane flung it to the ground with a muffled oath. "The damn thing could serve as a modern-day chastity belt!"

Carling began to giggle. She was excited, her nerves humming, her emotions very close to the surface. "I guess a bikini would be a bit more conductive to—uh—poolside romance."

"Definitely. Wear one next time." He laid her back onto the chaise and lowered himself over her.

"Sorry, I don't have one." She smiled up at him, opening her legs to him, for him.

"Then we'll have to buy you one, won't we?" His finger penetrated her, testing her readiness.

Carling closed her eyes and moaned. She felt as if she were on fire there, ready to explode with the wildness coursing through her body. "Kane, now. Please!"

She felt her body being stretched and filled. She clung to him, enveloping him. The emptiness was gone, he was part of her now. The pleasure was so intense it obliterated her awareness of everything else.

He thrust into her with increasing power, faster and harder and deeper until he felt her body convulse around him and she was whimpering soft, sexy sounds that she couldn't control. Her climax triggered his and he felt explosive shock waves jolt through him as he gave in to the wild, surging pleasure.

They lay together for a long while afterward, their bodies still joined. Carling felt the heat and hard weight of his body upon her, inside her. She smelled the musky male scent of his skin, and the heady aroma of sex. She sighed, savoring the supreme contentment, the sublime glowing warmth.

"Kane," she whispered his name, just to say it, just to hear it on her lips. She wanted to say something more, something profound that would convey the way she was feeling. Alas, her verbal creativity seemed to have taken a leave of absence. She didn't know what words she wanted to use. She really wasn't sure what she wanted to say.

Kane slowly sat up, and she had to force herself not to beg him to stay with her.

He stared at her, his eyes intent. Her eyes were heavy lidded, her lips moist and parted. She wore the expression of a woman who had been loved to rapturous satisfaction. Just knowing that he could make her feel that way, could make her look like that, made him feel like the most potent, desirable male on the planet. He wanted to say something to convey the way he felt when he was with her, the way he felt about her, but he couldn't. He didn't know what words he wanted to use. He really wasn't sure what he wanted to say.

For a few long moments, they stared at each other, saying nothing. Then Kane heaved a ragged sigh, picked up his swim trunks and put them back on. "Ready for your first swimming lesson?"

"Now?"

"Now."

"I guess so." Languorously, Carling stretched and sat up, her movements slow and sensuous. She was very aware that he was watching her. And then she noticed her suit, all rolled up and tangled on the ground.

"Uh-oh," she said with a grimace. She didn't want to go through her fat-lady-and-the-girdle routine again. It had been ungainly enough when Kane's eyes had been clouded with passion. To have him view the performance now was out of the question.

His gaze followed hers to the suit. A wicked smile slashed his face. "Perhaps you'd like to take the lesson nude? It can be easily arranged. Your instructor is very obliging."

"I'm sure," Carling said dryly. "If you'll excuse me for a moment, I'll go inside and find another suit to put on." She reached for her canary-yellow terry cloth cover-up and slipped it on.

"While you're inside, take a minute and order the bikini from that catalog you were poring over."

She looked at him with surprise. "You noticed?" She was slightly unnerved. It wasn't as if she'd been drooling over the pages. In fact, she thought she'd been rather subtle.

"I notice everything about you, Carly."

His tone, firm, quiet and exceedingly seductive sent tiny ripples of heat tingling through her. But she remembered her vow not to spend his money on anything for herself but necessary health-care products. "I have more than enough swimsuits, Kane. I don't need a bikini."

"If your other suits are all like that rubber armor lying there on the ground, you definitely do need one, Carly. Anyway, you wouldn't have mentioned it if you hadn't wanted one. Order it."

"I can't."

"You can't? Why is that?"

She took a deep breath. "Kane, we'll never be able to pay back the thousands and thousands of dollars that you gave to my father. I have no intention of adding to the Templeton debt."

"The Templeton debt," he repeated carefully. "You're really hung up on that, aren't you? I've already told you— how many times?—to forget it. There is no debt."

"I can't forget it," she said. "How can I when it's changed my whole life?"

If Kane hadn't given her father that money, she wouldn't be married to Kane, she wouldn't be standing here right now, warm and wet from his loving, she wouldn't be wondering if she was pregnant with his child—because she was already a week late.

She could never forget how she happened to become Kane's wife, because it was a fact of their history. But it was a fact that was beginning to matter less and less, she realized with a start. What seemed important now was that they were married. She was his wife and maybe nine months from now, the mother of his child!

But Kane wasn't privy to her thoughts. He reacted strictly to her words—and they were fighting ones to him. "So we're back to that, hmm?"

His eyes blazed with sudden, fierce anger. He'd come to hate it when she threw up to him the conditions of their marriage. Perhaps his methods had been—well, a bit unorthodox—he was forced to concede. Still, the end result had been a marriage that was working out very well, so didn't the successful result justify the means?

He wasn't an avid proponent of the "end justifies the means" school of thought but, in this case, there was a valid argument to be made for it. Carling was happy as his wife and he knew it, though she might be too proud and too stubborn to admit it. And he ... well, he was happy too. Happier, in fact, than he'd been in years. Maybe even in his entire life. *He* wasn't too proud or stubborn to admit it, at least to himself, he added with silent self-righteousness.

And then it hit him—what he wanted, what he expected from her. The impossible. He wanted her to forget the peculiar history behind their wedding, to consider their marriage as one which had been entirely, mutually voluntary. To act as if they'd met, fallen in love and decided to marry, just like any other couple.

Kane scowled. What an idiot he was! Carling had made her feelings about this marriage—and him—perfectly clear from Day One. Sure, she responded to him physically. After all, she was a passionate young woman whose warm and loving nature had been suppressed for too long. He was good in bed, he was skilled in the arts of arousing a woman, he had sexually awakened her. There was definite chemistry between them, but he was foolishly deluding himself if he thought that his wife was a willing partner in this marriage anywhere else but in the bedroom.

A surge of fierce primitive rage coursed through him. That he knew his anger was unreasonable made him even angrier. His mouth tightened. "Since you seem determined to wallow in the image of yourself as a bought-and-paid-for slave, I won't try to argue you out of it anymore. From now on I'll speak to you as your master, not as your husband. When I tell you to buy something, you'll damn well buy it, just as you'll do what I tell you to do, wear what I tell you to wear." He smiled coldly. "Need I continue or do you understand the concept?"

Carling stared at him nervously. He was furious! This was the first time she'd ever seen Kane truly angry, and it was more than a little scary. No matter what she'd said or done previously, he had reacted with insouciance or amusement or occasional mild exasperation, but never this rage she now saw burning in his eyes. He was so big and strong. The size and strength of him coupled with his anger underscored her own weakness and vulnerability.

The caustic retort she would normally have flung at him died on her lips. His wrath had a definite dampening effect on her own. Instead of exploding in rage at his infuriatingly chauvinistic declaration, she decided to beat a strategic retreat.

"I'd like to go inside now," she said, striving hard for a detached composure she was far from feeling. Implicit in her cool withdrawal was the fact that she wouldn't be back out for a swimming lesson.

"Then go inside," Kane said harshly. "And think about what I told you."

Carling fled into the house. Even his tone scared her. What a wimp she'd become, she thought dispiritedly. The old Carling would have never let anyone speak to her so imperiously.

But she was no longer the old Carling, she admitted, as foolish tears misted her eyes. Worse, she didn't want to be the old Carling again, and that revelation was scarier than anything Kane could have said or done to her.

They avoided each other for the rest of the day, meeting only at dinner which they ate in cool, tense silence. Afterward, Kane tossed down his napkin and rose decisively from his chair.

"I'm going over to the Wayne ranch to talk to Sam Wayne about a foal he's interested in buying from me," he said, heading out of the room.

Carling felt her heart stop, then start again at triple speed. He couldn't go to the Waynes; Holly was supposed to be there with Sam and Edie's son Joseph. She wasn't, of course. Edie Wayne's disclosure that afternoon made Carling certain of that.

The scenario unfolded unpleasantly in her imagination: Kane, already in a bad mood would go to the Waynes, expecting to find Holly and Joseph. He would make some remark and the loquacious Edie would mention how much time the young couple spent at the Triple M. She might even mention having thanked Carling for tolerating their presence. Then Kane would know that she had helped Holly deceive him.

Carling shivered. She didn't even want to think about what kind of a mood he would be in when he returned home. There was something more, too, something she wasn't ready to acknowledge: she didn't want Kane to think that she'd betrayed him. She wasn't yet up to facing what that said about her feelings for Kane.

"Kane!" She blurted out his name as she scurried after him down the hall.

He paused and turned to face her. "Yes?"

Carling was really nervous now. Anything she said would plunge her deeper into this stupid, involuntary conspiracy with Holly. "I—I don't think you should go."

"And why not?"

"Because . . . people shouldn't go storming away in anger. It's not—" She paused, frantically searching her brain. What was the word she was looking for? "Very nice."

This was a sophisticated public speaker? Carling mocked her own insipidity. But an angry Kane McClellan unnerved her more than a raucous political audience numbering in the hundreds.

"Too bad," Kane said coolly. "As a slave you have no input concerning any of my actions."

"Would I have some input as your wife?" she shot back.

He started walking toward her. "What are you trying to say, Carly?" He came to a stop directly in front of her.

"I—I'm not sure. Maybe that I want to be a wife and not a slave?" Her words surprised herself as much as they surprised Kane.

"That would mean that you'd have to stop all that nonsense about adding to the Templeton debt." He put his hands on her shoulders and she raised her head to meet his eyes. "You'll have to—"

"Spend your money?" she interrupted, a teasing glint in her eye. Their fight—or whatever it had been—was over. She knew it, and she suddenly felt giddy and lighter than air.

"You'll need it for such necessities as bikinis and lingerie and bunny rabbits for that infernal collection of yours that's taken over the den." A slow smile curved the corners of his mouth. "But we'll have to negotiate the amount which—"

"Oh, I know, I know, you've already explained the McClellan Rules of Shopping to me." She lowered her voice, mimicking his. "Shopping is not a vocation to us. We buy what we need when we need it but—"

"Maybe my lecture was somewhat patronizing and paternalistic," Kane conceded.

"I think obnoxious and offensive are the words that best sum it up."

"Is that so?"

She nodded. "Kane?"

He took both her hands in his. "Hmm?"

"Is it too late to have a swimming lesson now?" She forgot all about the Waynes and Holly and why she couldn't let Kane go there. Foremost in her mind was mending the rift between them—and just being with him. If that also included learning to swim, so much the better.

"The pool is heated and lighted. We could do it if you wanted to."

"I do."

"Okay, then. Let's go." He flung a casual arm around her shoulder and they headed to their bedroom to change.

Halfway down the hall, Carling's arm crept around his waist and her head came to rest lightly in the hollow of his shoulder. It seemed natural for the two of them to walk together that way, normal for them to glance at each other and spontaneously smile. And oh-so-right for him to draw her into his arms as they stepped inside their room for a long, deep, passionate kiss.

Ten

Kane was delighted when his younger brothers, Scott and Tim, arrived for an impromptu weekend visit the following Friday, the day before he, Carling and Holly were scheduled to have dinner with the Waynes. Carling and Holly weren't at all surprised by the visit. They knew that the Waynes had invited the boys to the enormous party they were throwing to honor the newlyweds and to welcome Carling to the county. Wisely, the logistics and the size of the party were being surreptitiously kept from Kane.

Carling couldn't remember exactly when she'd begun to consider Kane's aversion to big, bustling social events amusing rather than annoying. Her change in attitude seemed to have evolved naturally. After all, she reasoned, Kane wasn't a genuine misanthrope. He had friends he enjoyed seeing, either one-on-one or in small groups. However, he was selective about whom he chose to spend his time with—and she knew that she was one of the chosen.

Kane would rather be with her than with a roomful of guests, regardless of how charming or illustrious or useful they might be. That appealed to her, although she wasn't ready to put a label on why and how she found his attention and preference for her so affecting. And stirring. And arousing.

Kane proudly introduced Carling to Scott and Tim, indulging in some big-brotherly bragging. In just a few weeks, Tim would be graduating with highest honors from Rice University, and a trip to the graduation ceremony was already scheduled. Immediately afterward, Tim planned to move to New York, where he'd been accepted into medical school.

"I wish you could take some time off and relax here at the ranch for a while, Timmy," Kane said, eyeing his youngest brother warmly.

Tim laughed. "I couldn't sit around with nothing to do any more than you could, Kane," he teased. "I'm ready to get moving. I can't wait to get into my new apartment and start my classes."

"Kane's clone, the boy wonder," Scott muttered under his breath, too low for Kane to hear. But Carling was near enough to pick it up. She knew Holly heard too, because the young woman gave Scott a sympathetic smile and nodded her head.

Carling watched the brothers closely after that. Kane was obviously as proud of Scott and he was of Tim. She listened as Kane talked on at length about Scott's job at the bank in Dallas, about the fascinating ins and outs of the financial world. But it seemed to be a one-way conversation. Scott volunteered only a word or two about his job or about banking and finance. He seemed to have nothing to say about his social life, either.

Of course she had had no experience with sibling relationships, Carling reminded herself. Maybe it was the norm for the eldest brother to do all the talking. She noticed, though, that it wasn't that way between Tim and Kane. Tim was bursting to tell Kane everything, about his classes, his mates, his interests and activities, while Scott shared virtually none of the details of his life in Dallas.

Different personalities, different styles of relating, Carling told herself, as she walked to the stables where the horses were kept. She'd taken to visiting there every other day or so, though she kept her visits a secret from everyone. She had no intention of getting on one of those four-legged snorting giants but she'd decided that she ought to at least learn to tolerate their presence. Anyway, she thought the baby horses were cute, even petting them if their mothers kept a respectable distance.

Her determination to conquer her fear of horses had nothing to do with any desire to befriend the species or to learn to ride, even at a slow trot. But she was *not* going to be one of those mothers who infect their children with their own foolish fears and hang-ups.

And she was going to be a mother! Carling wavered constantly between awe and disbelief at the realization. She was eight days late—an extraordinary phenomenon in a body that had always been as regular as clockwork—and so she'd purchased a home pregnancy testing kit at the drugstore in Stanton. The results had been positive, but Carling hadn't quite believed it. A baby growing inside her? She thought of how badly she'd wanted a baby sister or brother throughout her childhood. Now it seemed she was to be gifted with a baby son or daughter of her own.

After two weeks, she'd bought another testing kit, just to be certain. Once again, the results were positive. She really was pregnant!

Now she was three weeks and four days late, well into her first month. It was time to think about making an appointment with an obstetrician. Carling laid her hand on her abdomen. It had become an automatic gesture lately, as if she were protecting and comforting the tiny new life growing inside her. She was filled with a serene contentment, a peace and calm that she'd never before experienced in her peripatetic life as a Templeton.

She hadn't told Kane about any of this. She was consumed with the wonder of having a baby inside her, so very proud of that amazing accomplishment. But every time she thought of telling Kane she grew anxious and uncertain. It was *her* baby and something in her balked at sharing her secret with him.

There was no use pretending that they were a normal married couple or that Kane was a husband madly in love with his wife, pregnant or not, Carling reminded herself bleakly. Though she'd ceased to refer to herself as his bought slave, the facts hadn't changed. Because her father's political future was completely in his power, Kane McClellan owned her. She was a hostage, held in exchange for her father's career—and so was her unborn baby.

Carling quickly put the thought from her mind. It was too painful to think about a child hostage, a baby of blackmail. Her eyes filled with hot tears. She was so emotional these days, so confused. Only one thing seemed inviolate as long as she kept her secret, her child was free.

The barn door was open and Carling walked inside heading automatically for Winsome's stall. Winsome seemed less threatening than the other horses; she didn't glower and make menacing noises when Carling approached, the way some of the others did. One time she could have sworn the horse had nodded with maternal approval when Carling had stroked and cooed to Winsome's beautiful little foal.

She passed the stall of her nemesis Lady Slipper, and jumped when the horse made a sudden movement toward her. She was annoyed with her own skittishness and when Lady Slipper emitted a jeering whinny—yes, it was definitely a jeer—Carling stuck her tongue out at the horse.

She stopped when she heard Holly's voice, and then Scott's, and was about to call out a greeting when she heard them mention her name. Immediately, she fell silent. Then

as an old saw about eavesdroppers never hearing anything good about themselves, but Carling doubted that it
had ever hindered a potential eavesdropper from listening
in. It certainly didn't hinder her. She leaned against the side
of one of the stalls, out of sight, and proceeded to listen
shamelessly.

"I just don't know how to tell him, Holly!" Scott exclaimed. There was genuine anguish in his voice, and resentment as well. "Since he's married to Carling, I was
hoping he would concentrate exclusively on her, but he's as
involved in our lives as he's always been."

"That's Kane for you," Holly said gloomily. "Always
ready, willing and able to run the lives of the people he loves.
He simply added Carly to his list."

"I never thought Kane would marry. He must be crazy
about her," Scott said thoughtfully. "Can she get around
him? Could we use her as an ally?"

"I'm not sure. She's crazy about him, too. Right now I'm
living in mortal fear that she'll tell him what she thinks she
knows about Joseph Wayne and me."

Scott and Holly thought that she and Kane were crazy
about each other? Carling felt another ridiculous rush of
tears fill her eyes and she mocked herself for her own stupid sentimentality. It was true what they said about emotions running amok in pregnant women, she decided.
Otherwise, why should she feel like crying because Holly's
and Scott's supposition *wasn't* true?

"Oh, Scott, what's the matter with us anyway?" Holly
was wailing when Carling tuned back into the conversation. "We're nothing but spineless cowards! We deserve to
have our lives run by Kane because we let him do it. We
never stand up to him."

"How do you tell someone who's devoted his life to you,
who gave up all his own plans and dreams for you, who
wants only the best for you and is absolutely certain that he
knows what will make you happy..." Scott paused to draw

a deep breath. "How do you tell him to butt out and let
live our own lives?"

"We don't." Holly sighed. "Instead, we lie and snea
around behind his back. We're worse than cowards, Scot
We're genuine creeps. It would serve us right if someho
Kane were to find out the truth. In fact, I almost wish
would."

Living in the political arena wasn't unlike life in the th
ater, and Carling had learned the value of good timing ar
the merit of a dramatic entrance. She used both to full a
vantage when she stepped from her hiding place to jo
Holly and Scott. "How would you like your wish to con
true, Holly?"

Holly shrieked. Scott jumped. Both gaped at Carling
if she were an apparition.

"Were you spying on us?" demanded Scott. "Did Ka
put you up to it?"

"How much did you hear?" Holly wanted to know.

"I'm not a spy and all I heard was that you two consid
yourselves a couple of lying, sneaking creeps." Carlin
shrugged. "I don't happen to agree with you, but if you fe
that way, why don't you tell Kane whatever it is you can
bring yourself to tell him and stop the lying and the sneal
ing."

"Oh yeah, right." Scott laughed sardonically. "Tell Kan
who thinks banking is the world's greatest career, that I d
spise it? Sure, Carling. Kane pulled all kinds of strings to g
me that job and I know some ambitious banker type wou
kill to be in my position, but every day I spend in that ban
is like doing time on death row."

Carling thought of how proud Kane was of Scott's bud
ding career at the bank. Hadn't investment banking bee
Kane's first choice of a career for himself before his pa
ents' fatal accident had compelled him to return to the ranc
and raise his younger brothers and sister?

"Surely it isn't written in stone that you have to be
banker, Scott," she said reasonably. "That might've bee

Kane's aspiration for himself, which he transferred to you, but if you tell him how you feel, don't you think he'll understand? There are so many careers and you—"

Holly and Scott interrupted her with laughter. It wasn't a happy, full-of-fun kind of laughter, either. Carling swallowed. She was seized by a sense of ominous foreboding. "What career do you have in mind, Scott?"

"I'm a rock singer with a band," Scott exclaimed eagerly. "The lead singer. I play guitar and keyboard and have written some songs. We've been booked at college parties for the past three years and have started getting regular weekend gigs at clubs in Dallas and Fort Worth. We want to go to L.A. But I have to grow my hair," he added, running his hand through his short, banker-style cut with a look of genuine disgust on his face. "And I need to get at least one earring. You can see how having to look the part of a staid banker is really hurting my rocker image. I have to wear a wig when we play!"

Though Carling wasn't an expert on the latest heavy metal rock bands, she knew enough about them to know that they were undoubtedly the antithesis of the conservative sedate banker, style-wise, personality-wise, in any and every way.

"You want to be a rock star," she said flatly. She remembered when she was five or six years old, she'd wanted to grow up to be a princess. It struck her that Scott's career goal was on a par with that. And he was twenty-four!

"It's not like this is some wild pipe dream and I don't have a prayer of making it!" Scott argued, as if reading her mind. "I have talent and I work hard at my music. All I need is one good break. And I'm gonna make it happen. I quit the bank yesterday and I'm heading for L.A. this weekend, right after the Waynes' party. I—I'll tell Kane then."

"Oh no!" Holly exclaimed in dismay. "Why didn't you give me advance warning? I could've arranged to be visiting my college roommate in Atlanta and missed what's going to be an explosion that'll rival a hydrogen bomb."

Carling tended to agree with her. She knew only too well that Kane was used to having things go the way he'd planned them to go. And he was accustomed to having people do what he wanted them to do. Having Scott trade a promising banking career for an electronic guitar and an earring was not viable in the world-according-to Kane McClellan.

"How will you support yourself in L.A., uh, until your big break, Scott?" Carling asked politely. She fervently hoped he wasn't expecting Kane to foot the bill. Because she knew he wouldn't and she didn't want to see the brothers' relationship ruptured.

Strange, she'd once wished Kane a life of misery—she'd even promised him one!—but now that he was facing disappointment and possible estrangement from his brother which she knew would make him truly miserable, she could hardly bear the thought. She wanted to protect him—a ludicrous notion since Kane was so tough and so strong that he seemed to need protection from no one.

Scott heaved a sigh. "Don't worry, I'm not counting on my big brother to subsidize me. Not that he would, anyway. Kane believes in hard work and making it on your own. Our father was in debt and the ranch was going to hell when Kane took it over and made it profitable—and made a fortune from his sideline interests, too. He could've easily kept it all to himself, but he set up trust funds for Holly, Timmy and me. We're financially secure, but we won't get a penny of the money until we turn thirty. Kane wanted us to *have* to learn to support ourselves, not be rich kids living off money we hadn't earned ourselves."

"That was very wise of him," Carling said thoughtfully, remembering how aimless she'd been. She'd had too much time on her hands and no goals, responsibilities or ambitions. She wouldn't want her child to lead such a life.

"Of course you'd think so," grumbled Holly. "But if Scott had his money now, he could go to L.A. and live in style out there."

Scott shook his head. "No, Kane is right about the money. Besides, I can't buy myself a recording contract. I have to be good enough to get an offer. I figure I have six years to make it. If I haven't hit it big by the time I'm thirty, I'll go back to the bank and make my money work for me."

Carling smiled. Either she was getting accustomed to the idea of Scott as a rock musician or she was beginning to feel that his plans weren't quite as insane as she'd originally thought. She told him so.

"I wish Kane would see it your way, but there's not much chance of that," Scott said dolefully. "Will you help me break the news to him, Carling? Not until after the party, though. Let's keep it a secret till then."

Carling agreed and tried to think of ways to present his plan in the most favorable—or least horrifying—light as she walked back to the house with Holly and Scott.

"There is one question I'd like to ask, to sort of prepare myself, since you McClellans seem to have a penchant for secrets," she said. "Are Tim's graduation and plans for medical school for real? Or are they bogus? Does he have an undisclosed alternative ambition, something along the lines of living in a tent on the beach and becoming a full-time surfer?"

"Not Tim," Scott assured her. "He's not leading a secret double life. Tim has always been the most like Kane. Successful at whatever he tries. Up-front, honest, open and frank." He gave a self-deprecating grimace. "Unlike Holly and me, who want to please Kane but then end up double-crossing him."

"Not wanting to work in a bank is hardly a double cross," Carling said soothingly. "And just because Holly and Joseph want to be alone but are too embarrassed to—"

"Holly and Joseph Wayne?" Scott interrupted with a hoot of derisive laughter. "Don't tell me you bought the trumped-up tale, too! I thought you knew that—"

"Shut up, Scott," Holly cried fiercely. "If you say one more word, I'll go straight to Kane and tell him that you quit the bank."

"And I'll tell him that you've been carrying on with his ranch manager for the past ten months and using a phony romance with Joseph Wayne as your cover," snapped Scott.

Carling's jaw dropped. "The ranch manager?" she echoed. Webb Asher and Holly? She could hardly take it in. "But what about Joseph Wayne? His own mother said that he, that you—"

"Joseph and I worked out an arrangement because we both needed to get out and we knew our families would never object to a romance between the two of us," Holly said sullenly. "We could go out every night and stay out as late as we wanted, no questions asked, because Kane and Sam and Edie Wayne are positively enraptured with the idea of Joe and me as a couple."

"And all those times you were supposed to be with Joseph, you were really with Webb Asher?" Carling stared at the young woman in disbelief. "But why the subterfuge, Holly? Kane speaks highly of Webb Asher. He likes him. I can't believe that he wouldn't approve of your dating him."

"Dating him?" Holly repeated with a sneer and then promptly burst into tears. "I'm not *dating* him, Carly! I'm sleeping with him, every chance I get. He lives in the bunkhouse, but there's a partition around his bed so—"

"The bunkhouse?" Carling was appalled. She'd seen the bunkhouses, including the largest one with the paper-thin walls partitioning the ranch manager's sleeping area from the ten other bunks in the building. No wonder Holly had been so desperate for her own place in Stanton. Making love in the bunkhouse? Carling shuddered. "Holly, that is *not* a place anyone could ever consider conducive to romance."

"Romance?" Holly laughed hollowly, through her tears. "Webb isn't offering me romance, all he wants from me is sex. He doesn't love me and he's never pretended to. He sees other women and flaunts them. He doesn't ever want to marry and settle down."

"Webb is a throwback to the cowboys of the Wild West," Scott explained. "He likes to drink and fight and roam from place to place. He's been here for five years and is terrific at his job, but he'll probably move on just because he doesn't want to put down roots."

"He'll end up putting down roots in the cemetery if Kane finds out he's been using Holly," Carling said grimly. "At the bunkhouse!" She grimaced. The lack of privacy, the seediness, the smell . . .

Her mind was truly boggled. "Holly, why? I'll concede that Webb Asher is good-looking in a hard, rough sort of way, but you're so pretty and bright, you have everything going for you. Why would you accept such shabby treatment from any man?"

"Not any man, Carly. Just him, just Webb." Holy cried harder. "I love him, Carly. I love looking at him, I love touching him, I love the way he makes me feel. I'll do anything to be with him, whenever he wants me. Think of the way you feel about Kane . . . what if he didn't love you in return, what if he only wanted you for sex? Loving him the way you do, wouldn't you go to him whenever he called? Wouldn't you—"

"I have a strong feeling that if Kane were to invite Carling to the bunkhouse for sex, she wouldn't have any difficulty refusing his call," Scott interrupted dryly.

Holly stopping crying long enough to give her brother a sharp jab in the ribs with her elbow. Carling didn't blame her. This was hardly the time for humor. For Holly's words had stuck a paralyzing nerve within her: *I love looking at him, I love touching him, I love the way he makes me feel.* Didn't that accurately describe the way she felt about Kane?

Carling began to tremble as the revelation hit with full force. Oh God, I'm in love with him! She wanted to laugh and cry at the same time. Of course she was in love with him! There could be no other explanation for the feelings and changes within her, feelings and changes which she had refused to examine and acknowledge on anything but the most superficial level. But she admitted them now. Kane had become the center of her life; she loved him so much while he...

He didn't love her. Carling forced herself to face reality. The pain to her psyche was shattering, far worse than any physical pain she had ever suffered.

What if he didn't love you in return, what if he only wanted you for sex? Holly's description of her depressing relationship with Webb Asher also defined her marriage to Kane, Carling thought, and despair surged through her.

Kane didn't love her; he owned her and controlled her. At least when she'd thought she hated him, she had the strength and spirit to fight back, but now... Now she was pregnant and had admitted to herself that she was deeply in love with him. Now she ran the risk of being completely subjugated under his domination, because her love would make her weak, no match for the indomitable Kane.

She pictured her lost self, weak and cringing with no will of her own, afraid to speak her mind to Kane, to tell him when he was wrong—and dammit, he *was* wrong at times. What kind of a mother would such a shadow figure be? Her children might very well end up like Scott and Holly, mixed-up and deceitful, because they perceived Kane as an unapproachable tyrant, however well-meaning his motives might be.

She reflexively covered her still flat abdomen with both hands. Her child deserved a happy family with two strong parents, who respected and loved each other. Instead, it faced being stuck with a lovelorn wimp for a mother and an unchallenged dictator as its father! Her poor baby!

"Oh, Carly, don't cry." Holly put her arms around Carling and hugged her. "It's so kind of you to care so much."

Carling knew that Holly thought she was crying tears of empathy, not realizing that she was crying for herself and her baby and the unholy mess they were in. She'd fallen in

love with Kane, a man who didn't love, a man who owned
and controlled and always, always made things go his way.

"Well, you'd both better stop blubbering before Kane
sees you," Scott said with brotherly scorn. "Because then
we'll have to cook up a reason why you're both crying and
I don't know about you, but I'm not feeling very creative at
this particular point in time."

"We could always say that Joseph Wayne dumped me,"
Holly said, brightening a little. "Maybe then we could get
out of the party tomorrow—because it's going to be awful.
For the first time in my life, I'm going to hate a party as
much as Kane will. Webb will be there flirting with every
single woman in the county. And Joe and I will supposed to
be pretending we're in love, when nothing could be farther
from the truth."

"Since Joseph agreed to your charade, did he need a
cover for a secret lover, too?" Carling asked. She didn't
really care, but she'd always found making small talk was
easier than having to face her deepest feelings. Particularly
when they were so dismal.

"Poor Joey. His situation is even worse than mine,"
Holly said sadly. "He's in love with an American Indian girl
named Maya, a full-blooded Apache. She's a social worker
on the reservation about a hundred miles southwest of
town."

"And the Waynes hate Indians, especially Apaches,"
continued Scott. "I mean they really *hate* them. Prejudice
is too mild a word to use to describe their feelings. They'll
disown Joseph if he marries Maya and he really loves her.
She loves him too, but I think their relationship is doomed."

"That's terrible!" Carling cried, forgetting her own misery for the moment.

"Tom Wayne, Sam's great-grandfather got scalped during a fight with an Apache, so the story goes," said Scott.
"According to Kane, the rest of the story is that Tom Wayne
was a murdering, thieving cattle rustler, who got exactly
what he deserved. Of course, the Waynes don't see it that

way. They've been born and bred to hate Indians down through the generations."

"That's revolting!" Carling was indignant. "These are the 1990s, not the 1890s. There is absolutely no excuse for such misplaced animosity."

"Try telling that to the Waynes," Holly said grimly. "You can see why Joseph was glad to work out a cover story with me. But we're both buying time and we know it. Sooner or later, the truth will have to come out."

"How about delaying it, till I'm far away in California?" suggested Scott.

Holly glared at him. "Do you have to be so damned flippant?"

They began to bicker. Carling felt too drained to care. What a day this was turning out to be! She felt as if she were living in a maze of mirrors, which distorted everything. Nothing was as it seemed. Kane thought that Scott was happily employed in a Dallas bank and that Holly was in love with Joseph Wayne. He didn't know about their baby or that she loved him. He was existing in an entirely different reality and Carling found it difficult and confusing to maintain the pretense. There were too many things to keep straight!

It was easier to avoid Kane, and she did so, pleading an upset stomach and going to bed immediately after dinner. She pretended to be asleep when he came in to check on her several times throughout the evening. And when he climbed into bed beside her later that night, she kept her eyes closed and her breathing deep and even.

Kane moved closer and touched her arm. He felt the soft warmth of her skin and inhaled the feminine sweetness of her body. Every muscle in his body tightened; he was ready, willing and able to take her immediately. No one but Carling had ever affected him so intensely. All of his senses responded to the sight and sound, the smell and the feel of her. And his desire kept growing stronger, the longer they were together.

Desire had become need and he knew it. There was no use denying it. He was in love with her; there was no use denying that, either. But telling her... Did he dare? He was accustomed to examining and analyzing all sides of a situation before making an investment and he did so now. Tell her he loved her? When she didn't love him, when he'd forced her into marriage, disrupted her life....

It was all so new to him, being in love and feeling uncertain. It was unsettling to realize that he couldn't control Carling's emotions or his own. It was more than unsettling; it was downright terrifying! He resolutely tried to think about something else, anything else: the price of oil, the young bull he'd been wanting to purchase from Bobby Killeen's stud farm, Juanita's incomparable chicken-fried steak and milk gravy. But nothing diverted him for long. Carling claimed his thoughts as well as his heart and his body.

Was she pregnant? he wondered. He was fairly certain that she was. He was an observant man and as a result of his vested interests in cattle and horses, extremely knowledgeable about breeding. A slight smile curved his lips. He'd better not put it in those terms to Carling; she would definitely be insulted.

He wanted her to tell him that she was pregnant. Every day he waited and every day she didn't mention it. Was it possible that she was unaware of her condition? It seemed unlikely. Still, he'd rather believe that than face the fact that she was deliberately keeping the news from him.

Tonight she'd eaten a full meal, then said she felt sick. She'd looked fine but he hadn't questioned her when she insisted on going right to bed. He knew that fatigue and nausea were both common symptoms of pregnancy.

She was carrying his child! The thought filled him with such pride and love he thought he would explode. In fact, his aching, throbbing body was already perilously close to doing exactly that. Tonight was the first night since they'd been married that they hadn't made love and he wanted her so much he was shaking, from the urgency of his passion for her.

"Carly?" he whispered her name. When she didn't respond, he said it again, a little louder. Still, she appeared to be deeply asleep, not stirring at all, her breath coming in a slow deep rhythm.

And he knew then that she was faking. He knew that she awakened easily and quickly. He'd certainly awakened her often enough deep in the night, his body hard and burning for her. Now she was deliberately pretending to be asleep, not realizing that her comatose act had given her away.

"What's going on?" He hadn't realized that he'd spoken his thoughts aloud until he heard his voice break the silence in the room.

Carling's heart thumped and she rolled onto her stomach and buried her face in her pillow. Had Kane found out about Scott or Holly and their convoluted dilemmas? He would view her prior knowledge as complicity and she dreaded his disapproval as much as his wrath. She simply wasn't up to quarreling with him tonight. Even a calm discussion was too arduous to contemplate. She was exhausted, from the demands of pregnancy, from the emotional upheavals of the day—and from pretending to be asleep while lying there alert and tense.

"You can stop faking, Carly. I know you're awake. Do you feel like telling me why you felt the need to enact this little charade?"

She continued to lie still and made no reply.

"Coma victims are more responsive than you are. Give it up, Carly," he said roughly. His growing anger was a welcome diversion from the passion which still shook his body. "If you don't want sex, then say so. One thing I can't tolerate is dishonesty."

Carling's heart plummeted. If you don't want sex, he'd said. *Sex.* Not making love, but sex. That's all he wanted her for, for sexual release. He was like Webb Asher summoning Holly to the bunkhouse for a quick roll in the . . . bunk.

Which brought her to another sickening realization. One thing I can't tolerate is dishonesty, he'd said in a tone that meant it. And she was dishonesty personified, deceiving him by omission by not sharing her knowledge of Scott and the rock band, and Holly and the ranch manager, and Joseph Wayne and his Apache girlfriend. Not only did Kane not love her, he would find her presence intolerable when the truth came out.

It was too much to bear and her emotions were too fragile from the stress of early pregnancy. Hating herself as a weak-minded nitwit, Carling nevertheless gave into the sobs that racked her body. Tears streamed down her cheeks. She kept her face firmly buried in the pillow, swiftly dampening the pillowcase.

"Carly, what's wrong?" Kane sounded truly alarmed. He sat down on the bed and tried to take her in his arms.

She fought him, pulling away from him. She was too dishonest to deserve his comfort. But there was much, much more. She absolutely refused to be soothed by the man who had sex with her but didn't love her, who'd made her pregnant but didn't love her. Who'd made her fall irrevocably in love with him but who didn't love her.

"Go away, leave me alone," she sobbed. She managed to sound both fierce and heartbroken at the same time.

She was pregnant, Kane was sure of it now. He stared at her bleakly, and reluctantly withdrew from her. At any other time, he would have stayed and held her and petted her and aroused her until she was moaning and clinging to him, and the tension and hostility between them had been melted in the heat of their passion.

The rough, never-give-up-or-give-in part of himself urged him to do that now. But the protective, paternal part of him won out and he bowed to her wishes. She was pregnant and she knew it and she hated him for it. He was certain of that. It explained her withdrawal, her tears and rage. Never had he felt so low.

"I'll leave you alone," he said quietly. "I'll sleep in one of the guest rooms tonight."

He left the room noiselessly, closing the door behind him. Carling sat up in bed and stared around the empty room in shock. He'd left her! This was the first night of their marriage that he hadn't made love to her. No, it was the first night that he hadn't had sex with her, she mentally corrected, but as quickly as she'd had the thought, she discarded it with a shake of her head. Whatever it meant to Kane, to her it was making love. She was so in love with him.

She climbed out of bed and walked to the window, staring out at the moonlight and willing him to come back to their room. He wouldn't have to say a word; she would gladly give herself to him. She faced the unthinkable—that she would even make love with him in a *bunkhouse* if he asked her to!

She went back to bed and lay down. If he hadn't returned in fifteen minutes, she decided she would go to him, even if it meant searching all through the house to find him. Her eyes drifted shut. Fifteen minutes, she promised herself. And promptly fell asleep in five.

Eleven

She had attended her first party at the tender age of two weeks old, and had gone to countless others for the subsequent twenty-eight years, but none in Carling's memory came close to equaling the Waynes' party. It was by far the most traumatic, miserable, wretched event of her life, almost enough to make her detest parties as thoroughly as Kane did.

The day had started out badly enough. She'd awakened, alone in her bed, and learned that Kane had flown to Dallas. He'd gone without telling her he was leaving or when he was coming back, although he'd left word with Juanita, the cook, that Carling was to go to the Waynes for dinner with Holly and the boys and he would join them later.

By the time he arrived, the party was in full swing, with cars lining the entrance to the Waynes' house, instantly tipping him off that this was a social extravaganza, not the quiet family dinner he'd been anticipating. He hadn't seen Carling all day and he barely got to nod to her before he was swept away by a jolly band of well-wishers, leaving her to make mindless small talk with her new neighbors.

They were welcoming and friendly and eager to fill in Kane's lucky new wife on all the details of Kane's premarital life. "I can't believe that Kane finally tied the knot," a man named Bobby Killeen, about Kane's age, exclaimed incredulously. "I never thought he'd get married, not when he didn't marry Missy Howser. Now *that* was one hot and heavy romance! The whole county was keeping tabs on that one." He chuckled and rolled his eyes heavenward. "Did Kane ever tell you about the time he and Missy were in the midst of one of their humongous fights and to get even, she arrived at a party wearing one of those flouncy dresses and no underwear? And proceeded to take part in a square dance?" He grinned broadly at what was obviously a fond memory.

"No," Carling said with a tight smile. "He never shared that particular anecdote with me."

"Bobby, just hush up!" Bobby's wife glowered at him. "We're all sick to death of that story and Carling isn't interested in what is now ancient history."

Carling managed what she hoped was a lighthearted little laugh. Wasn't Missy the same old girlfriend who had constantly played that former favorite song of hers she was never going to listen to again? "Whatever happened to that Missy person, anyway?" she asked, feeling curious in spite of herself.

"Why, she got married and divorced and returned to Stanton earlier this year," Bobby replied. "There she is, over there, across the room. The great-looking brunette in the slinky black dress. Um, looks like she's just spotted Kane and is going over to talk to him."

Carling turned in time to see a voluptuous dark beauty slither to Kane's side and gaze up at him with worshipful black eyes. From the way the woman had been poured into her eye-popping, tight-fitting dress, it was obvious that she'd forgone her underwear tonight, too.

Carling glanced down at her own dress, which was bright ed cotton with white polka dots, had a fitted bodice, shirred elastic back and full swingy skirt. She didn't dare compare herself and her outfit to the sexy, sultry Missy; her ego wasn't up to such a challenge.

She escaped from the effervescent Bobby and his wife and moved on. T. R. Wayne, Joseph's older brother, and his wife Janie were eager to chat. They had nothing much to say about Missy Howser except, "We knew Kane would never marry that little tramp," but reminisced fondly about Robin Sue Taylor, with whom it seemed, Kane had shared another equally compelling "hot and heavy romance."

"Kane and Robin Sue broke up because she resented having to share him with the younger kids, and of course, Kane wouldn't hear of giving them up or sending them away," Janie said with a sigh. "I never thought he'd marry after that. From then on, he just sort of dallied with lots of different girls."

"Is Robin Sue here tonight?" Carling asked resignedly. Undoubtedly, she was, and looking gorgeous and sexy to boot. It was that kind of night, that kind of party. A party from hell.

"She sure is!" T.R. said heartily. "That's Robin Sue, over here, across the room. The knockout redhead."

"The one heading toward Kane," observed Carling. She felt jealous and depressed. There was no one in her dull, uneventful past whom she could claim as a former great love. Kane was the one and only true love of her life.

Standing here, watching two of Kane's ex-loves jockeying for his attention, was definitely one of the low points of her life, she decided miserably. She had to *do* something! She glanced desperately around the room and spied the Triple M's ranch manager, Webb Asher, necking with a giggly young blonde who had obviously had too much to drink.

Carling looked over at Holly, who was sitting beside Joseph Wayne on a corner sofa. Both looked so young and so

hurt. Joe was probably wishing the woman he loved wa:
here, accepted by his family. And Holly's eyes never lef
Webb, who was indeed flaunting his pretty young compan
ion.

Carling's blue eyes narrowed to slits and her mouth
tightened into a firm, straight line. She'd been looking fo
something to do and taking the perfidious Webb Asher to
task filled the bill perfectly.

"I want to talk to you," she said imperiously to him, ther
turned to the blonde and said in a tough, impolite tone tha:
she'd never used during her years as the senator's perfec
daughter: "Get lost."

The blonde stopped giggling and promptly disappearec
into the crowd. Webb Asher smiled his insolent smile. "Sc
what can I do for you, Carly? Get you a drink? Name you:
poison, babe."

The insect actually thought she was coming on to him!
Carling stared at him with distaste. "First, you will refer to
me, *always*, as Mrs. McClellan. And second, unless you're
prepared to marry my sister-in-law, you will stop seeing her
immediately."

Asher's jaw dropped. "You—you know about Holly and
me?" He looked totally disconcerted.

She'd taken him by surprise and Carling homed in on her
advantage. "I know everything. And the only thing stopping me from telling Kane right now is that it'll take a couple weeks to institute a search for a new ranch manager. A:
soon as—"

"Mrs. McClellan, I don't want to leave the Triple M.'
Webb Asher was perspiring now and had turned a chalky
white. "It's the best job I've ever had and the closest thing
to a home I've ever known."

Carling was not moved. "Then you know what you have
to do, don't you?"

"I can't get married. I'm not a marrying man!" he exclaimed, clearly in a panic at the very thought.

"Then break it off with Holly," Carling said coldly. "I'll be watching you carefully and if I find that you dare continue to use her for your—your own selfish pleasure, I'll fire you on the spot." She paused, to heighten the effect of her words. "And then I'll tell Kane everything and he'll make certain that you'll never work on a ranch anywhere, ever again."

She wasn't sure if Kane could actually carry out her threat, but Webb Asher seemed to think so. He lowered his eyes and stared at the ground, his shoulders slumped in defeat. "Yes, ma'am," he mumbled without a trace of his usual bravado.

Carling watched him walk away, knowing that Holly was going to be hurt by his rejection, yet feeling convinced that she'd done the right thing. Because she cared about her young sister-in-law, she just couldn't stand idly by and let her be used by an unfeeling rake.

She felt a hand close around her upper arm and gave a startled gasp. Threatening Webb Asher had been such a successful diversion that she hadn't noticed Kane desert his fan club and join her.

"We're leaving," Kane growled, "as soon as we say goodnight to Sam and Edie."

"Surely you haven't finished catching up with Missy and Robin Sue?"

Kane groaned. "I have great friends, but they talk entirely too much."

"But then, you've given them so much to talk about," she said sweetly. "Your reputation as a reclusive rancher is totally misleading—you're a romancing rancher. How many other former sweethearts do you have roaming around the county? And are they *all* here tonight?"

He frowned, his gray eyes darkening with controlled anger. "If you're trying to be funny, you might take note that I'm not laughing."

"I'm beginning to understand why you aren't too crazy about big parties," Carling continued, undaunted. "It must

be extremely inconvenient to have all the players in you
romantic past mingling with—"

"Forget Sam and Edie. We're leaving now." He pushe
his way through the crowd, his grip on her arm never slack
ening.

Ever well-mannered, Carling automatically smiled and
made her goodbyes as he dragged her along after him. N
one seemed to mind that the guests of honor were leaving
early. The other guests all kidded and laughed, as if they'c
expected it.

It was a silent drive home. Carling studied Kane co
vertly, trying to gauge his mood. How angry was he? She
tried to emulate his cool withdrawal but she couldn't sus
tain it. By the time they reached the Triple M, her nerve
were tightly strung. This was not good for a woman in he
condition, she scolded herself. She had to take care of her
self and the baby, and having an anxiety attack was hardl
prenatally ideal.

"Kane, this is making me crazy," she announced, as the
entered the dimly lit foyer. "I'm not spending another nigh
like last night."

"You slept like a baby last night," Kane retorted. "
know that for a fact because I came in to check on you te
minutes after I left the room." He grimaced wryly. "It wa
a resounding blow to my self-esteem to find you sounc
asleep instead of fretting over my absence."

She stared at him, her blue eyes wide. "Oh."

"Yeah." He shrugged. "Oh." He started down the hall
way. "Come into my office." It was a command, and sh
followed, too bemused to rebel.

When they were inside the paneled office, he handed he
a thick portfolio. "Everything is in there," he said in a cool
gruff tone. "The complete record of the financial transac
tion between your father and me. There is only one copy anc
when you destroy it, there will be no evidence of any ques
tionable financial dealings concerning Senator Clayto
Templeton."

She stared from the portfolio in her hand to Kane's hard, unyielding profile. What did it mean? Her mind clouded. She tried to think but couldn't.

"You're free, Carling," he said, as if in answer to her unspoken question. His voice was as forbidding as his expression. And he had called her Carling.

"Why?" she whispered. "Why are you doing this?" Her hand settled on her stomach, just above the place where their child nestled within her. Destroying these documents had been a dream and a goal of hers, but now that she had them in her hands, she couldn't decide if she wanted them or not. It all depended on what Kane's motives had been in giving them to her.

Pain shot through her sharp as an arrow as a horrible thought struck her. What if his offer of her freedom was really a ruse to get rid of her? "Did seeing Missy or Robin Sue tonight have anything to do with—"

"Oh, give me a break!" he snapped, glowering at her. "I flew to Dallas today to retrieve these documents. I intended to give them to you before I saw either Missy or Robin Sue at that damnable party. And you can't seriously believe that I'm even remotely interested in either one of them. I could have had them years ago if I'd wanted them. They wanted to marry me but I didn't want to marry either of them," he added with a trace of his usual Kane-like bluntness.

His voice lowered. "I didn't want to marry Missy or Robin Sue or any other woman, Carly. Just you. Only you. It's always been you and always will be. But I'm not going to force you to stay with me any longer. Your father's political career doesn't depend on whether you go or stay, not anymore. You're free to choose."

She clutched the portfolio. Her mind had cleared. She could see everything so clearly now. And what she saw made her heart pound with joy. "So this is my own personal Emancipation Proclamation?" An intense burst of love exploded within her. "You're saying I'm free to go if I please. You won't stand in my way or try to influence my decision in any way." Her mouth curved into a wickedly seductive smile and her blue eyes shone as brightly as twin stars. "You'll do or say nothing to try to make me stay."

"For godsake's, don't make it any harder for me to let you go," he said hoarsely. Carling stared at him in surprise. She'd been teasing him and he'd taken her seriously. It astonished her that he didn't realize what she was trying to tell him. Kane was usually so fast to catch on, so quick witted.

But the pain, which shadowed his face, had obviously dulled his perceptive powers. "What I did was wrong. Using my hold over your father to force you into marrying me was *wrong*, Carly." His voice was low and deep and filled with remorse.

Carling gripped the back of a chair and hung on. She was stunned. Kane McClellan admitting he was wrong? She thought back to their wedding day when he had informed her—with his customary blend of unshakable confidence and maddening arrogance—that marrying her against her will was a perfectly acceptable thing for him to do because he knew they were right for each other.

There had been a time when it would have galled her to admit that he'd been right all along. They *were* perfect for each other. And there was a time when she would have positively reveled in his admission of wrongdoing. But that time was past. They had both come a long, long way in a relatively short period of time. Love had reformed and redeemed them both.

"Are you telling me that you regret marrying me?" she asked quietly, knowing the answer, yet wanting to hear him say it.

"No!" he exclaimed fiercely. "Marrying you is the best thing I've ever done. I love you, Carly. I love you so much I..." His voice trailed off and he stared moodily into space. "I want you to love me, to stay with me and live with me as my wife because you want to, not because you—"

"Were bought and paid for?" Carling filled in, trying but not quite succeeding in stifling a mischievous grin.

He gave her a long, penetrating stare. She could almost see *his* mind clearing. She could feel the relief and the happiness that he was feeling as he realized the truth. That she was free to choose and that she'd chosen to love him.

He pulled her into his arms for a long, hungry kiss, holding her, loving her with a passion that would never be extinguished.

"I love you," Carling whispered when he lifted his mouth from hers. "Oh, Kane, I love you so much." Tears began to trickle down her cheeks, and she wiped them away with an apologetic smile. "I'm sorry. Lately, I seem to cry all the time, whether I'm happy or sad or mad."

He smiled down at her. "Mmm, and why is that, do you think?"

She drew back from him, linking her arms around his neck and gazing into the gray depths of his eyes. His hands moved over her waist, her belly, with loving possession. "You know about the baby!" she exclaimed.

"I wasn't sure if you did. I've been waiting for you to tell me."

She sighed happily and snuggled closer to him. This had to be one of the sweetest moments of her life, she thought, and was not at all surprised when her eyes filled up again. "I'm pregnant, Kane. I bought two of those kits at the drugstore to be absolutely sure." She hugged him tight. "And don't you dare mention anything about *breeding cycles*," she added, looking up at him with laughing, loving blue eyes.

"Not a word, I promise." He leaned down to kiss her again, and then asked seriously, "Are you happy about the baby, Carly? I wanted a child right away, but I never asked you. It's something we should have discussed before I made you pregnant, I realize that now."

"Next time we will," she resolved. "But I'm thrille
about having this baby, Kane. There is something I'd lik
you to promise me, though."

"Anything, darling. Name it."

"I want you to help me be the kind of parent I want to be
You know, give our kids plenty of love but also the free
dom to be themselves. If I ever get the urge to mold ou
children into perfect little campaigners for Grandpa, pleas
remind me of this conversation. Likewise, if they try some
thing once and it doesn't work out and they feel scared an
nervous about trying again, help me to convince them tha
it might not be such a bad idea, after all."

"You're going to be a wonderful mother, Carly, the best
And I promise to be the best father I can be."

"The kind of dad who would be supportive and not an
gry if we have a musically talented son who decides he'd lik
to be a rock star instead of, oh, working in a bank?"

"Hmm." Kane considered it. "If he was young and ha
already completed his education and didn't have a wife o
family to support, I guess I might be—" he cleared hi
throat "—can we leave it at, not totally aghast?"

"That'll do for now. And if we have a daughter who get
involved with the wrong man, you wouldn't lecture her
you'd do everything to ease her heartbreak, wouldn't you
And if we have a young neighbor who falls in love with a
Apache and his family hates Indians, you'd do your best t
convince them otherwise. And you'd succeed, too," sh
added lovingly. "Because Kane McClellan always does."

His brows narrowed. "Exactly how hypothetical are thos
situations and those kids?" But then she smiled at him an
nothing else mattered except that she loved him, that sh
wanted to stay married to him of her own free will and tha
she was going to have their child.

"What the hell, together we can face anything," he sai
in a lighthearted tone far removed from his usual respons
ble, serious mode. "Here, open the present I bought you i
Dallas."

He handed her a big gift-wrapped box which she quickly opened. "Rabbits!" she exclaimed in delight, removing each individually wrapped piece of porcelain. She set them on his desk, one by one. "A rabbit wedding!" She was thrilled. "A bride and a groom, bridesmaids and a best man, and even a little flower girl and ring bearer." She threw her arms around him. "Oh, Kane, they're wonderful. I've never seen anything like them!"

"Believe me, neither have I," he said dryly. "I saw them in a gift shop window in Dallas this afternoon. Normally, I avoid gift shops the way you avoid horses, but I had to go in and buy them." His eyes gleamed with laughter. "A bunny rabbit wedding set somehow seemed—symbolic."

"You're right," she said breathlessly.

His fingers were already tackling the long zipper in the back of her dress.

"Of course. I'm always right." He swept her up in his arms.

"Except when you're wrong," she said, kissing the firm, strong line of his jaw. "But don't worry, I'll be here to tell you when you are. I love you, Kane. I love being married to you and I'm going to love raising our family."

"I was right about that," he said with satisfaction. "We belong together, Carly. I knew it would work out."

She began to unbutton his shirt. "Are you going to take me to bed or stand here gloating?"

They were in the bedroom within thirty seconds flat.

*   *   *   *   *

proudly presents
the long-awaited "prequel" volume of

★ LOVE AND GLORY ★

by
LINDSAY McKENNA
Dawn of Valor

In the summer of '89, Silhouette Special Edition premiered three
novels celebrating America's men and women in uniform: LOVE
AND GLORY, by bestselling author Lindsay McKenna. Featured
were the proud Trayherns, a military family as bold and patriotic
as the American flag—three siblings valiantly battling the threat
of dishonor, determined to triumph... in love and glory.

Now, discover the roots of the Trayhern brand of courage, as
parents Chase and Rachel relive their earliest heartstopping
experiences of survival and indomitable love, in

Dawn of Valor, Silhouette Special Edition #649.

This February, experience the thrill of LOVE AND GLORY—from
the very beginning!

DV-1